Praise for *Evil Eye*

"Exquisitely suspenseful. . . . The relationships between the damaged, sometimes monstrous individuals who people these pages will keep the reader riveted."
—*Publishers Weekly* (starred review)

"With her focus on deviant and twisted characters, Oates continues to be a worthy descendant of the gothic tradition of Edgar Allan Poe." —*Kirkus Reviews*

"[Oates is] the ultimate horror writer. . . . She rivals Dostoyevsky in her understanding of the darkest elements of ordinary people."
—Huntington News

"This is familiar Oates territory, mapped with artistry and care; dark, bloody, and unforgiving." —Barnes & Noble review

"Immediately engaging . . . [the] suspense is palpable."
—*Shenandoah*

"A quartet of shrewd and unnerving novellas. . . . Oates has a superbly disconcerting gift for orchestrating slowly coalescing realizations that something is horribly wrong." —*Booklist*

"A proper definition for the word *love* is as slippery and ambiguous as the future of Oates's seemingly doomed characters. . . . Oates makes the reader feel as if an evil eye is trained upon them with the passing of each hour and the turning of each page."
—*Missourian*

Also by Joyce Carol Oates

EVIL EYE

FOUR NOVELLAS OF LOVE GONE WRONG

JOYCE CAROL OATES

The Mysterious Press
an imprint of Grove/Atlantic, Inc.
New York

"So Near Any Time Always" appeared in *Ellery Queen Mystery Magazine*.
"The Flatbed" appeared in *Conjunctions*.
"The Execution" appeared in *Fiction*.
"Evil Eye" appeared in *Boulevard*.

Published simultaneously in Canada
Printed in the United States of America

ISBN 978-0-8021-2288-9
eISBN 978-0-8021-9402-2

The Mysterious Press
an imprint of Grove/Atlantic, Inc.
154 West 14th Street
New York, NY 10011

Distributed by Publishers Group West

www.groveatlantic.com

14 15 16 17   10 9 8 7 6 5 4 3 2 1

for Lucy and Gil Harman

Contents

EVIL EYE

1.

It had belonged to his first wife, he'd said.

First wife so casually uttered—she, who was the *fourth wife*, could have no basis for misinterpretation.

That is, no basis for hurt. For envy, jealousy. Even, the husband seemed to suggest, in the almost negligent way in which he spoke of the *first wife* to whom he'd been married *a lifetime ago, when we were other people*—curiosity.

And so, she'd known not to ask about the wife.

"It's a *nazar*—a talisman to ward off the 'evil eye.' You see them everywhere in Turkey, Greece, Iran—also in southern Spain, where Ines was born."

She'd first noticed the strange sculpted-glass object when she'd first entered the house of the man whose *fourth wife* she became within a year of their meeting. But there were so many striking and curious objects in the sprawling stone-and-stucco house amid fragrant eucalyptus trees, so many primitive masks and sculptures, exotic wall hangings, silk screens, "shadow puppets" —she'd been too intimidated to inquire and had stared in silent appreciation, like one who has stepped into a museum unprepared.

She was so much younger than the man: the proper tone to take with him was deferential, acquiescent.

And she would learn from him, for he was a man with much to instruct.

The *nazar* did resemble an eye, though not a human eye: it was rimmed with dark blue, not white, and it was flattened and not spherical. And it was large, and lidless, blank and staring, about eight inches in diameter, conspicuously hanging beside one of the arched doorways of the dining room that led to the kitchen at the rear of the house.

When you looked more closely you saw that the *nazar* was comprised of concentric circles: the wide dark blue outer circle, a narrow white inner circle, a pale blue circle, and, at the center, a small black "pupil." The dark-blue glass was particularly beautiful, luminous, when sunshine streamed through it in the morning.

"Educated people in those countries don't exactly believe in the *nazar,* or in the 'evil eye'—but they wouldn't tempt fate by defying it. There's a Turkish airline with the *nazar* on its planes, for good luck."

She thought *In the matter of luck, we need all we can get.*

She thought possibly she'd seen these Turkish airplanes, in European airports. But she hadn't known what the *nazar* had meant at the time. She said:

"It's very beautiful. And uncanny—an eye without an eyelid."

"Well, it's been here forever. Since Ines moved out, in 1985. I've stopped noticing it of course. But if someone removed it, I would."

Even the uglier objects in her husband's house exuded an unsettling sort of beauty, Mariana wanted to believe she would grow into.

Soon after this conversation, though there could have been no direct connection, Austin informed Mariana that Ines was coming to visit.

Ines? For a confused moment, Mariana had no idea whom her husband meant.

Austin Mohr knew so many people: so many people knew *him*.

In their first weeks, months, now nearly a year they'd been together he'd told her about so many people who were prominent in his life, or had once been prominent, she couldn't keep most of them straight: *Suzanna, Harry, Darren, Felix, Michael, Cynthia, Enid, Jared, Henry, Florence, Ines* . . . These were professional associates, adult children and relatives, close friends, former close friends, former wives. At these times her husband spoke with such intensity, in so riveting a way, Mariana listened with the desperation with which a lost child might listen to an elder instructing her in a kind of code all that she must know to find her way back home.

Sometimes, despite her attentiveness, Mariana blundered.

"Excuse me, Mariana—'Henry' isn't my married son who lives in Seattle, that's 'Harry.'"

Or, with a frown, "Not 'Susan' but 'Suzanna'—my daughter in Shanghai whom you have yet to meet."

After the initial startled moment Mariana did recall Ines. Of course—the *first wife*.

"Ines rarely comes to the States and she will only want to see us—to stay with us here—one night. That has always been her custom. She'll come with her sister's daughter Hortensa—a nice girl, a gifted cellist, if not very attractive. Don't look so dismayed, Mariana —Ines isn't a difficult person. She may look like a *prima donna* but she isn't, really. If you don't let her intimidate you, she won't."

Mariana tried to smile. Mariana was feeling a clutch of panic.

The *first wife* coming to visit—to stay with them!

In her parents' household, which was the only household Mariana had known intimately, it was inconceivable that either her father or her mother would have invited a guest to stay with them without consulting with the other.

Or was it two guests, including the niece?

Of course, they were living in her husband's house. In which he'd lived for more than thirty years.

And Mariana was grateful to be living here. Often, the thought came to her like a mild electric shock—*Grateful to be living. Here.*

For her own life had collapsed, shattered like broken crockery.

"I wish you would smile, Mariana. Ines is no threat to you—or to me, at this point in my life. Our breakup was amicable. I've sent Ines money over the years only because she's careless and heedless of her life, not because it's required of me any longer. And when she comes to the States, it has been a custom of mine—of ours—for me to ask her how she's doing, financially; and if she tells me frankly that she needs money, I will give her money. But only if she asks."

Austin spoke matter-of-factly. You could not tell—Mariana could not tell—if his tone was one of regret, or equanimity.

Hesitantly Mariana asked: "Ines didn't remarry?"

The husband laughed, as if Mariana had said something sardonic or witty.

"No! Certainly not. After me, Ines never remarried."

The new wife, the *fourth wife*, was thirty-two years younger than the *first wife*, who was two years older than the husband.

The gap of years was like a fissure in the earth, treacherous only if one tries to leap across it.

As the *fourth*, so much younger wife, Mariana felt no triumph, but rather more a guilty sense of having usurped another woman's place.

It was astonishing to Mariana how casually her husband spoke of his former wives: "When we were traveling in the Amazonian rain forest"—"When we were making a documentary on Chinese opera, in Beijing"—"When we were staging a full-cast

Mahagonny in Edinburgh." The *we* was undefined, mysterious, like the ages of Austin's several adult children and where exactly they were living and what they were doing.

Mariana had been relieved: not one of her stepchildren had made the journey to attend their father's wedding. And the wedding had been small, private—a brief civil ceremony.

She'd been so happy at the time, her heart so suffused with wonder, her memory of the actual ceremony, in a small local courthouse, was hazy.

One of Austin's children had died, Mariana knew. An infant son, who hadn't lived a year.

Ines's infant, this had been. Long ago in 1983, two years before Mariana was born.

How strange it was, how unnatural it seemed, that a man and a woman might share such a tragedy, as well as other, so-intimate experiences as a husband and wife, and not be bound together for life, like Siamese twins. The very term *breakup* seemed so crude, cruel.

Mariana's parents had been married for more than thirty years. They'd been "older" parents—her mother had been forty-one when she'd been born.

She wondered what her parents would have thought of her marriage to Austin Mohr. She hoped they would be happy for her, that she would be protected now that they'd left her.

She tried not, in the most primitive and childlike of ways, to blame them. For they were blameless.

And so it left Mariana breathless, the way in which her husband so calmly spoke of the past as if it were utterly and irrevocably *past*.

When they'd first met, Austin had told her of his several marriages, his wives—"Each very different, and each very wonderful. For a while." He insisted that each divorce had been "amicable" but Mariana wondered if that could be so.

Glass walls, skylights, beautiful airy rooms looking out at the city and the Bay miles away, glittering at night—who would willingly leave this house? And the social distinction of being Austin Mohr's wife, though that hadn't mattered in the slightest to Mariana—surely this would be a terrible loss for most women?

Often Mariana had to interrupt Austin to ask, with an apologetic laugh, "But wait—which wife are you talking about? When was this?" and Austin would say, "That's not the point of the story, who happened to be with me then. It isn't *who* or *when* that's crucial, darling."

She was rebuked in her superficiality! She was made to feel very *young*.

She was rebuked for thinking, with a tinge of inward pain—*But if I love you so much, am I not crucial to you?*

It was disorienting to think, to be instructed, that the *personal* wasn't just ephemeral but insignificant. That, in the rich tapestry of Austin Mohr's life, no single individual could matter very much—except Austin Mohr.

Yet she was captivated by the merely personal, like one who has stumbled into quicksand. At a less vulnerable time in her life she hadn't been so focused upon the intimate, the domestic, the *we* as she was now; for now, nothing seemed really to matter to her except the *merely personal*.

Where one lived, and with whom; the fact that one was not abandoned and lonely. *That* was what mattered.

Of course Mariana knew: set beside the cultural, the political, the aesthetic, and the moral, the *merely personal* is trivial and vulgar. Austin was right: why did the *we* matter, in the Australian outback, for instance? Or in a consideration of Chinese opera? When *we* included young children, on a trip to India in the 1990s, why did the specific identity of the children matter?

In her parents' lives, Mariana had mattered so profoundly. She couldn't help but feel that they'd abandoned her by dying—prematurely. Though it was ridiculous to think so, of course.

Austin had assured her, he would love her as her parents had loved her except more—"As a husband. Our bond is deeper."

Mariana had married a distinguished man. A quasi-public man. Austin had been the director of the Institute for Independent Study in the Performing Arts, in San Francisco, for more than a quarter-century; his name was legendary, in some quarters—"Austin Mohr." And now Mariana was *Mrs. Austin Mohr*, if she wished to be so designated.

Austin thought that "married" names for women were ridiculous. Of his wives each had retained her maiden name and had never been *Mrs. Mohr*. Each had been, he'd said, a woman with a life of her own independent of his; each had had her own work, her career.

Mariana felt a touch of jealousy at her husband's pride in his ex-wives' *careers*.

Her own career, such as it was, seemed to have been derailed since her marriage. Even before her marriage, her work had been stalled for months.

"You don't pay any of your ex-wives alimony, then?"

"No longer."

"Child support?"

"No longer, of course—my children are all grown."

"But I meant, when they were young."

"When they were young, often my children lived with me. They traveled with me. Sometimes their mother would come with us, on a trip. Former wives need not be former friends. Even if we rarely see one another, like Ines Zambranco and me."

Ines Zambranco and me. The words gave Mariana a chill.

Austin misunderstood Mariana's look of distress. He took her hand, kissed it in a way both playful and concerned.

"Don't look so stricken, Mariana—please! Ines and I are no longer emotionally engaged in the slightest. It's even an exaggeration to say that we're 'friends,' I suppose—since we have virtually no contact with each other except these occasional visits of hers. She comes to the States to see other people primarily—not me."

Ines wasn't the mother of Austin's adult children, Mariana gathered. The second and third wives—she was always confusing their names—were the mothers of his several children, whom Mariana had yet to meet.

"I am not obliged to pay any of them anything, any longer. So—don't give it a thought, dear Mariana!"

Mariana was ashamed to have provoked this exchange, which made her appear venal, small-minded. In fact she scarcely cared about her husband's financial situation.

She cared only that he loved her. That her love for him, as outsized in her life as the double bass she'd once carried on a city bus to and from music lessons, was not unreciprocated.

Austin said: "Ines was an actress when we met, but not ambitious as you must be to succeed in that life. She'd been very beautiful when she was young, like Catherine Deneuve—whom in fact she knows. She still acts on Spanish television mostly, in minor roles. Her last film role was in a Merchant-Ivory film, I forget the title. It didn't do well, though it starred Jeanne Moreau—another woman friend of Ines's." Austin paused, stroking Mariana's hand. It didn't discomfort her that he treated her at times like a convalescent; she took solace from his concern for her, for she knew it was genuine.

At the Institute, in his public guise, Austin Mohr had to be attentive to many people, in his warm, gregarious manner. If he failed to smile, a heart might be broken. If he seemed to forget a name, or a face—a heart would certainly be broken. But with Mariana, in the privacy of their home, his emotions were frank, sincere.

"As for Ines—she's a particular sort of Hispanic woman: emotional, but coolly so. Emotions, too, can be premeditated—rehearsed. Ines likes to stir emotion in others, like tossing a match to see where it will land. She's reckless and headstrong and has made some unfortunate mistakes in her life but on the whole she's quite happy I think. In her world, *Ines Zambranco* has a small renown. You know about our son, I think?"

Austin's ebullient tone was subsiding. There was no way for him to speak of this new subject except somberly.

"Your son? Yes, you've mentioned. . . ."

Or maybe Mariana had heard. One of the facts of Austin Mohr's life repeated by others, who scarcely knew him, in hushed tones as one might speak of a great man, wounded.

"He was four months old. His name was Raoul. He was put to bed by his mother, in his crib—in this house. When we'd first moved in, before the house was renovated and an entire new wing added. The room—the baby's room was adjacent to ours, with a door between. That room doesn't exist any longer—you won't see it. Ines lay the baby in his crib for a nap—a quite ordinary nap—and he never woke up."

Awkwardly Mariana said: "I'm so sorry. . . ."

"Ines discovered him. She'd been out of the room only a few minutes, she always claimed. But it had to have been more—a half hour, at least. We had a Danish au pair girl but she had the afternoon off. I was—away. Ines hadn't really wanted a baby and she'd had a difficult pregnancy. She'd been just starting to get good film

11

offers, and pregnancy and a new baby sabotaged her career. I think it was a Polanski project she'd had to decline—just a supporting role; but the pregnancy happened, she didn't 'believe' in abortion, nor did I—at that time, in such circumstances. Yet after Raoul was born, Ines was devoted to him, though very superstitious, wearing amulets against the 'evil eye' on a silver anklet. Ines also cultivated a neurotic fear of the number thirteen—do you know there's a word for this phobia, which isn't uncommon?—*triskaidekaphobia*—as if that could explain anything! There was—there is—no explanation for this sudden infant death—'crib death'. . . ." Austin spoke rapidly, as Mariana had never heard him speak before. His ruddy face was damp with perspiration and heat seemed to exude from his fleshy chest. He'd been pacing about the room and now he seemed to have wandered out into the corridor just as a phone began to ring in his study; Mariana didn't know if she should follow him into the study. She thought *But this happened twenty-five years ago.* But she thought *I am his wife, I must comfort him.*

But when she caught up with Austin in his study he'd thrown himself into a leather swivel chair in his usual way and was laughing into the phone. When Mariana tried to touch him he pushed her away without glancing at her.

"Henry! Bloody hell! Are you still in—is it Dubrovnik?"

Quickly Mariana retreated. Such conversations Austin had with old friends could last a long time.

And she had preparations to do: Ines and the "cellist" niece were due to arrive in two days, the first houseguests of Mariana's married life.

*   *   *

"Mariana. You must not be alone for now, my dear."

So Austin Mohr had told Mariana, simply. And so it was.

She'd been midway through her first-year residency as a fellow at the Institute when her life collapsed.

First her father had died in December. Then her mother had died in early March.

The first death had not been entirely unexpected, but it had come far more swiftly than anyone might have predicted: Mariana's father had had surgery to remove a malignant growth from his prostate, but he'd contracted a hospital infection from which he had never recovered.

Mariana had had to leave the Institute to spend time with her grieving mother. She'd taken work home with her to Connecticut and immersed herself in her work as a distraction when she wasn't in her mother's immediate company. Gradually, her mother had seemed to be recovering—she'd urged Mariana to return to San Francisco. But after Mariana returned to the Institute in early March, her mother had a collapse of some kind, possibly a mild stroke, followed a week later by a massive stroke that had killed her.

The stress of grief Mariana was told.

Your mother has died of a broken heart.

Mariana wondered if her mother's use of prescription drugs had contributed to her death. Barbiturates to help her sleep, tranquilizers to help her endure the day, sometimes washed down with the remains of her husband's small cabinet of whiskey and bourbon.

Neither of Mariana's parents had ever drunk much. The bottles were old, dating back for years. Yet several had obviously been depleted. Mariana told no one, nor did Mariana's mother's doctor or anyone in the family bring up the subject.

Now Mariana, too, was stricken in the heart. Her grief was sharpened by her sense of incredulity—*This can't have happened! Both my parents . . . gone.*

Wandering her parents' house as if looking for them. Yet in terror of glancing into a room and seeing them.

Once, after her father had died, she'd happened to see her mother—forlorn, hesitant, standing just inside the doorway of her bedroom, staring at something in the palm of her hand which, as Mariana approached, she'd quickly hidden in her fist, thrust into a pocket of her rumpled bathrobe.

Pills, Mariana supposed. She'd pretended not to see.

And now it was a shock to Mariana to discover herself so —*weak.*

Yet she was determined to tell relatives that she was fine. She did not need their help, she was fine.

Like a zombie, barely functioning only when she was in the presence of others, Mariana had lived in her parents' house for several weeks, having taken a leave of absence from the Institute. There was so much to do, so suddenly—the list of "death duties" was endless—and she had so little energy with which to do it. And when finally she returned to the

Institute, her soul had seemed to have drained from her body. When she forced herself to come to the Institute, to sit at her computer in her carrel as she'd done previously, with such enthusiasm, now she was unable to work; she was unable to concentrate; she avoided her colleagues, her new friends, and stayed away from Institute seminars, for the effort to speak to others was too great. Her thesis adviser spoke of her situation to the director of the Institute, who summoned Mariana to see him at once.

She'd thought *He will tell me to quit. He will see I am hopeless.*

What a relief this would be! Eagerly then Mariana would follow her mother, as her mother had followed her father. All this seemed premeditated, utterly natural.

Certainly, Mariana couldn't complete her first-year project by May 15, she would tell the director. Nor did she see much point in requesting an extension because at the present time, she didn't see much point in completing the project.

How insignificant Mariana's work seemed to her now, what had been so thrilling to her before her father's death! She'd come to the Institute with the intention of examining archival materials relating to the films of Ida Lupino in the 1940s and 1950s: Lupino, a Hollywood actress, but also one of the first American women film directors. In the Institute archives were drafts of screenplays, personal notes, journals, letters, countless photographs and snapshots. But Mariana no longer had energy for research; the effort of examining stacks of faded typescripts and handwritten letters and pictures held together by frayed rubber bands, all of this quasi-precious material related to individuals dead for decades, was too depressing. Her discovery was that this first, gifted woman director was a pioneering feminist whose films depicted the Male as the demonic *noir* figure, and not, as usual, the Female—but even this discovery seemed trivial to her now, in the face of her terrible loss.

When Austin Mohr saw Mariana hesitating in the doorway to his office, looking as if she were about to faint, quickly he rose to his feet and came to her. "'Mariana'—is it? Come in, please."

He'd heard about her parents, he told her. He offered his condolences.

Immediately he said of course she could have an extension through the summer at least, to complete her project. That was understood: there was no need for her to file a formal request.

Mariana was stunned. She had not expected such a sympathetic reception.

She wasn't pretty—she wasn't sexually attractive. She'd never thought so.

And now in the aftermath of her parents' deaths her skin was deathly pale and her cheeks thin, her eyes raw-looking, bloodshot.

Her dark chestnut hair, which was usually wavy and glossy, falling past her shoulders, was limp, wan, in need of shampooing. Her fingernails were broken and uneven and ridged with dirt—her clothing had grown too large for her, unflattering on her lanky frame.

She'd lost ten to twelve pounds: she weighed hardly more than one hundred pounds, at five feet six.

In a kindly voice altogether different from the public personality that was eloquent, playful, and "witty," Austin Mohr asked Mariana about her parents. Her father, her mother.

Gravely he listened as she spoke. And tentatively, then with more emotion, Mariana spoke as she had not spoken since her mother's death.

Stumbling, faltering. Trying not to cry. But telling Austin Mohr something of what had happened, that still seemed to be unbelievable, unfathomable.

He asked her about how she was taking care of herself.

Mariana had no idea how to reply. Her *self* was of little interest to her now, a flimsy remnant of a time now past, extraneous, worthless.

"It's a dangerous time for you now, Mariana. The pull of the 'other' is so strong."

Mariana knew that Austin Mohr meant *the other world*.

"You must not be alone, my dear. I hope you know that."

Mariana wept, pressing a wadded tissue against her eyes. Austin Mohr spoke gently yet forcibly.

"We all have losses we think we can't survive. And sometimes, some of us can't. So we need help. We need emergency help. I will provide you what I can of 'emergency' help—first, I will cancel the rest of my appointments for the afternoon."

"But—"

"Of course. I will. I have."

"Just talk to me. Tell me more about yourself. Your work. Why you'd come to the Institute last fall. We have many applicants, you know—we can accept only one in ten—and so you're very special to us, Mariana. To me."

Mariana hadn't known she'd had so much to say, or the energy with which to say it.

It was said of the director of the Institute that in addition to the numerous essays and books he'd written on the subject of twentieth-century cinema, both American and European, he'd virtually memorized classic films and could recite long passages of dialogue. And so it seemed to Mariana that Austin knew as much, or more, about the *noir* films of Ida Lupino as she herself knew. He succeeded in distracting her from her grief to discuss the directorial strategy of Lupino's major films, as well as an obscure *Twilight Zone* episode Lupino had directed called "The Masks" in the 1950s. Together, Mariana and Austin analyzed the parable-like plot of this TV drama in which craven individuals at Mardi Gras in New Orleans are obliged to don masks whose ugly features reveal their inner selves—and, when they remove the masks at midnight, their faces bear the imprint of the ugly masks.

"It's a brilliant little moral fable, worthy of Poe. The mask deforms the face—the mask reveals the soul. So convincing is Lupino's presentation of the fantastical material, it hardly seems surreal. And hardly like typical television in the 1950s or even now."

Mariana was amazed that Austin knew so much about her thesis subject, that others thought to be obscure if not of questionable relevance. And that he seemed so clearly, so sincerely to care about her.

Though he was somewhere in the vicinity of sixty Austin spoke with the animation of a young person excited by films. Almost, there was a kind of naïveté in the man's enthusiasm, Mariana recognized as very like her own, until recent months.

Austin Mohr was a large gregarious man with gingery-silver hair still thick, wiry. At times—though not today—he wore this slightly long hair in a little ponytail, or pigtail; he had about him a Latino sort of swagger, though he didn't have Hispanic features; he wore crisply ironed dazzling-white cotton shirts open at the throat, showing tufts of gingery-silver hair on his chest. His eyes were alert, intense, unnerving in their intensity. On his left wrist was a large beautifully designed watch, on his right wrist a bracelet of small gold links.

Mariana's hands were limp and chill. Austin held her hands, and warmed them. Like a fussing father he murmured to her, chided her. "I insist—you must not be alone right now. And you must take better care of yourself. I will see to that, my dear."

Mariana hadn't been comforted in such a way since childhood. She felt her stiffness melt, a physical melting, she began to love the man then, love for Austin Mohr swelled in her, the first *feeling* she'd had since the news had come to her shortly before Christmas, her father was gravely ill, comatose, and would probably not ever regain consciousness.

In the early evening Austin drove Mariana to his house in the Berkeley hills, and prepared a meal for her, a classic chicken tajine made with dried fruits, almonds, couscous. It had been weeks—months—since Mariana had been able to eat a substantial meal, but she found herself eating now, hungrily.

In Mariana's family, men rarely prepared meals. It was touching to see this man in his kitchen, taking time, *taking care*.

They ate outside at a wrought iron table on the deck of his house overlooking the glittering city of San Francisco, the Bay and bridges. Mariana had never tasted such delicious wine—a Spanish wine, Austin said. A chardonnay.

The wine, the exquisite food, the view of the glittering city framed by eucalyptus branches—Mariana had to shut her eyes, the sensation of joy came so strong.

Maybe. I will live after all.

Austin drove Mariana back to her rented apartment, miles away. He walked with her to the door, steadying her. He didn't come inside but gently gripped her shoulders. Mariana lifted her face, prepared her numbed lips to be kissed—but Austin only brought his lips to her forehead, lightly as one might kiss a child.

"Good night, my dear Mariana! This is a beginning."

All that night she felt the invasion in her blood, as of a virulent infection.

A small fever beginning to rage. But of course this was not an invasion of malevolent bacteria, but love.

* * *

Within a week, Mariana was having dinner with Austin Mohr each night, usually alone with him.

Within six weeks, Mariana spent most nights at Austin Mohr's house.

And within six months, they were married.

2.

"Mariana. What the hell have you *done*."

She'd been so taken by surprise, so unprepared for a sudden flaring of anger in her husband of just a few weeks, she'd thought at first that Austin must be joking.

Mariana had been preparing the house for an evening reception following a film screening at the Institute, moving furniture, repositioning chairs, making a wider pathway to the outdoor deck. She'd carried the lacquered Japanese screen to another part of the living room, placed a set of Catalan bowls on a wall shelf where there was less chance of their being broken, and moved one of the more savage-looking African masks to a less conspicuous corner of the room. Several exquisite orchid plants in ceramic pots she also moved out of harm's way. But when Austin saw what she'd done, instead of being pleased with her as she'd hoped, he'd stared at her in disapproval.

"I suggested that you help prepare for the reception, before the caterers arrive. Not that you dismantle my house."

My house. Mariana was too shocked to fully absorb this.

"I'm sorry. I didn't—I thought . . ."

Mariana stammered an apology but Austin seemed not to hear.

"Have you been thinking, since you moved in here, that the way this house is furnished hasn't been carefully considered? Does it look to you as if things have been randomly thrown together? With no aesthetic logic? That my taste is inferior?—inferior to *yours*?"

Austin spoke in a voice heavy with sarcasm. Mariana was frightened, disoriented: it was astonishing to her that her husband, normally so civil and good-natured a man, a man with an effervescent sense of humor, should fly into a rage over her having moved a few things in the living room—such a trifle!

Murmuring *Sorry, sorry* Mariana hauled the Japanese screen awkwardly back to its original position. The lacquered screen had seemed to her a beautiful artwork, ebony-black stippled with small cream-colored butterflies and birds, at six feet just slightly too tall for its position in the room, but now Mariana could scarcely bear to look at it. Austin continued to rage as Mariana returned the Catalan bowls, the African mask, the exquisite orchids—(she was terrified that orchid petals would fall, being jostled. For some of the flowers were past their bloom)—ignoring the alacrity and humility with which his young wife undertook to correct her mistake.

Even now a part of Mariana's brain assured her *He isn't serious! He can't be serious. This is so petty . . .*

"I'm sorry, Austin! So sorry. I wasn't thinking . . ."

"Obviously. You weren't thinking."

How was it possible, Austin was still furious with her? After she'd apologized profusely and returned everything to its original position? Yet his eyes glared with a piggish intensity, his fleshy-ruddy face was suffused with blood. Austin couldn't have been more angry, more disgusted, if Mariana had defaced and broken his precious possessions—yet nothing had been damaged in the slightest. Why did he continue to be so angry? Mariana shrank from him, afraid that he might hit her. For the thought came to her, a swift warning *If he hits you once, he will hit you again. It will be the end.*

Badly she wanted to turn and run from the room, and out of the house—she had her own car, she could drive away. . . . The marriage had been a mistake: she must escape. But she knew she must not turn her back on this furious man, she must not insult him further. Though she'd never had any experience quite like this in her life she understood that Austin's fury had to run its course, like wildfire. If she did nothing further to provoke it, but maintained her attitude of abject apology and regret, the fit would subside, eventually.

She tried to recall quarrels she'd had with men. Young men: lovers.

But none had been anything like this, provoked by something so innocent and trivial. None had been so one-sided.

None had left her feeling so frightened and helpless. So alone.

Austin went to examine the orchids. There were six plants of about twenty-four inches in height, in ceramic bowls. In a small atrium in the living room were other exquisite plants—bonsai trees, a jade plant with glossy leaves, a three-foot lemon tree. Initially Mariana had wondered if these beautiful living things had been left behind by her most recent predecessor or whether they were Austin's; since she'd moved into the house, care of the plants seemed to have fallen to Mariana.

Finally, Austin stormed away, into his study. And Mariana was left behind trembling.

He hates me! That look in his eyes.

He doesn't love me after all. It has all been a masquerade.

"Stupid! But I will learn."

She was the *fourth wife*. She could not bear to think that there might one day be a *fifth wife*.

The variable *y* in the equation in which *x* was the invariable.

It had been reckless of her, unthinking, stupid—to have provoked her normally good-natured husband to such a display of temper. She had herself to blame, wholly.

And that unnerving look in Austin's eyes, as of sheer loathing: no recognition of the young wife whom he'd claimed to adore.

Just that look of murderous fury—this was quite a surprise.

Yet, set beside the terrible surprises of her parents' deaths, it was hardly devastating. *I can live with it. I will!*

Austin's previous wives had failed to accommodate this temper, Mariana supposed. But their expectations of marriage had to have been far different from hers.

Of course Mariana understood, when she thought about the situation more calmly, that there had to be *another side* to Austin Mohr. No one can be universally admired all of the time, as Austin seemed to be at the Institute; no one can be continuously *good, rational. Sane.*

When Mariana had first arrived at the Institute she'd been impressed with how everyone seemed to admire Austin Mohr. He'd acquired a kind of mythic status: *generous, kind, brilliant.*

She'd half-expected to hear that yes, of course, Mohr was "flirtatious"—or worse—with young women at the Institute; he'd been involved with theater and filmmaking all of his adult life, surrounded by attractive, ambitious young women, so this had seemed inevitable. Yet, Mariana hadn't heard anything disturbing about Mohr; he had no reputation for exploiting women, and no reputation for flying into fits of rage; though it was said of Mohr that he could "lose patience"—he "didn't suffer fools gladly"—these were very minor qualifications.

Presumably, Mariana's predecessors had felt the sting of his terrible temper. Very likely, his children.

Which is why they've fled him. All of them.

It was the unpredictable nature of Austin's moods that disconcerted Mariana. She'd vowed not to provoke him—she would not ever make such a mistake again, interfering with his possessions, in his house; but there were other, equally trivial errors she might make, addressing him in a way he interpreted as overly familiar, in the presence of others; in the kitchen, when they were preparing a meal together, making a suggestion to Austin about the recipes he was considering—innocently and naively as if she and Austin Mohr were on a par, and Austin Mohr not the more experienced cook.

And a terrible blunder she'd made, naively preparing a side dish of spinach one evening without consulting Austin, because spinach was a food Mariana thought might complement the seafood marinara recipe Austin was preparing; Austin had been furious, as if Mariana had insulted his judgment—"The meal I'm preparing is complicated, and complete, without any need of a 'side dish.' I can't imagine what you're thinking, Mariana. Why you would want to *interfere*."

It was very like tossing a lighted match into flammable material—a sudden explosion, a fire burning out of control.

Mariana offered to throw out the spinach, which enraged Austin all the more.

Mariana felt ill as Austin raged at her in the close confines of the kitchen that was, to Mariana, usually so warmly attractive a room, with a wooden butcher block table, dark red floor tiles, framed posters of Picasso and Matisse lithographs on the walls. Arteries stood out in Austin's sweaty forehead like writhing worms. Though Mariana apologized repeatedly, desperately, yet Austin continued to rage at her. She was baffled why such petty incidents made him so furious—she couldn't help but feel that possibly he was joking—but of course Austin wasn't joking but was deadly serious, slamming pots around, grinding his teeth in fury. That very day at the Institute there'd been an open debate about a controversial project and Austin had spoken calmly, clearly, and forcibly, without any suggestion of irritation or annoyance, still less childish rage. As if, in the intimacy of private life, in the close physical intimacy of marriage, another Austin Mohr flourished, reveling in excesses of infantile emotion, not to be repressed.

It must be all women he fears and loathes—I am only the current woman.

And sometimes, in their lovemaking—in which Austin was invariably dominant, always initiating lovemaking and always designating when lovemaking was completed—Mariana's husband exhibited a willful, even reckless impulsiveness, which left Mariana baffled and chagrined rather than hurt. (For lovemaking was so much *less personal* than other forms of engagement. In lovemaking, Mariana had no doubt but that her widely experienced husband scarcely recalled which wife, or which mistress, he held in his straining arms.) But their lovemaking passed almost entirely in silence and so the particular hurt might be more readily forgotten.

If Mariana whispered *I love you!* to Austin, often he'd drifted into sleep and could not respond. His sleep was heavy, sweaty, labored; his breathing was hoarse and irregular; like a waterlogged body Mariana thought him, floating just beneath the surface of the water. . . .

The thought of Austin's death terrified her. Her throat closed up, the thought was so awful.

Oh but I love you! I love you. . . .

Yet how strange it was to Mariana, that Austin seemed deaf to her apologies. She had never met anyone who seemed so resolutely *not to hear*. It hardly mattered if Mariana gave in immediately, admitting her mistake and apologizing, as if in his fury Austin was remembering previous experiences with women in which he'd been thwarted, insulted, betrayed.

She wondered if he blamed the first wife, Ines, for the son's death. Maybe that was it: he could not forgive the woman, he was not even aware of his rage for her, that spilled over onto Mariana.

She was so lonely sometimes! The mad thought came to her, she would become pregnant, despite the man's precautions: she would have a baby, that she would be less lonely.

But now, how wounding it was to Mariana, a soft-spoken young woman who had never learned to assert herself, still less to defend herself—the way in which her husband glared at her as if he loathed her; the very man who, in the early weeks of their romance, had gazed at Mariana with eyes soft with love.

That love she'd believed—-she'd *known*—to be genuine.

Now she didn't know what to believe. Her husband would "love" her again—but could she believe him?

It was as if Austin saw, in Mariana's place, an ever-shifting female form, diaphanous, unpredictable, and untrustworthy, that fascinated and enraged him by turns. He did not see *her*.

Already in this first year of marriage Mariana had thought several times that the marriage must be over. Her husband had had enough of her—was finished with her. He'd looked at her with such disgust, dismay, incredulity, rage—he'd actually clenched his fists as if he'd have liked nothing better than to strike her.

She'd wanted to flee the house. It was a beautiful house in a beautiful setting and yet—Mariana was coming to hate it.

Flee the Berkeley hills, so beautiful and yet so treacherous—the tight-curving narrow roads, hardly more than single lanes, rising into the steep misshapen hills, in which more than one center of gravity seemed to draw one downward, vertiginously; all of Panoramic Hill, as it was called, a fire hazard, obviously—for no fire trucks could make their way on such twisting roads.

It was earthquake terrain, too. When Mariana mentioned this fact, Austin laughed dismissively.

"The world will end, too, one day. Fortunately, I don't plan on being here."

Here was *I*, and not *we*. In his careless fantasy of the apocalypse, Austin wasn't including any wife.

After one of Austin's outbursts Mariana was sure that Austin would let her go. And she wasn't sure that she really wanted to remain with him, in so precarious and unstable a marriage.

Then again she thought, chilled, *Without this man, I am nothing. I am a daughter/orphan. I don't exist.*

After the spinach incident they'd had a strained dinner together on the deck overlooking the Pacific sunset: Mariana hadn't dared to speak, and Austin had scarcely glanced at her. He'd been preoccupied with other thoughts, that Mariana supposed had little to do with her, who'd entered his life so relatively recently.

He will tell me to leave. Is that what he told the others? It's over, please leave. This is my house.

But that night, when she was preparing to sleep in one of the guest rooms, and not in their bedroom, assuming that Austin didn't want her anywhere near him, there came Austin storming to the doorway to rebuke her.

"What kind of game is this! My wife belongs with me, in my bed."

My wife. In his state of supreme disgust Austin seemed to have forgotten Mariana's name.

"Hel-lo! You are Mariana—the new wife?"

The query was in such heavily accented English, the glamorous white-haired woman's expression so droll and curious, like that of an animated Kewpie doll, Mariana had a fear that she was being mocked even as the woman thrust out her small-boned beringed hand to shake Mariana's hand.

"I am Ines Zambranco, and this is my niece Hortensa."

"Yes—hello . . ."

"Unless—we have come early? Is Austin not ready to see us? Hortensa and I can go away somewhere and return a little later of course—if you would wish this."

Mariana had hurried to answer the ringing doorbell and was breathless. It was so, Ines Zambranco and her niece had arrived more than an hour early, and Austin was in another part of the house, changing his clothes.

Mariana stammered, "Of course, come in—please. You're not at all early . . ."

"But I think yes, perhaps we are? Hortensa and I, we have come by taxi, you see. From the airport. And it is not possible to time an arrival perfectly, in such circumstances."

"No, oh no—of course not. Please . . ."

Mariana was smiling nervously at both women—too confused to shake hands with Ines's niece who was standing beside Ines on the front stoop, a head taller than Ines, just slightly behind her, like a servant, burdened with a shoulder bag, a tote bag, and a large roller-suitcase. Mariana was trying not to think *They have come early deliberately. They want to unsettle me.*

Mariana looked from Hortensa back to Ines: this time, Mariana nearly fainted.

The gaily chattering Ines Zambranco was missing an eye. Where her right eye had been there was an empty socket.

It was a profoundly shocking moment: for you were led to look from the left eye, which was expertly made up, enlarged with eye shadow in shades of mauve and taupe, and outlined in black mascara, to the missing eye, where you saw what appeared to be a shadowy emptiness; your instinct was to look back at once to the left eye, that was gazing at you, alert with consciousness, and with a kind of merriment as well, as if the little white-haired woman with the missing eye, perfumed and elegantly attired as she was, knew perfectly well what you were thinking, what a shock you'd had—though of course, smiling fixedly at her, determined to behave as if nothing were wrong, you would not acknowledge the missing eye.

Yet—Mariana could not prevent it—she glanced back at the empty socket, which had been made up with cosmetics as well, black mascara outlining the socket's edge and an arched eyebrow penciled in above, a subtle combination of white, gray, pale brown that matched the other perfectly drawn eyebrow. The effect was both sinister and glamorous—for Ines Zambranco was a dramatic presence, looking much younger than her age of more than sixty, with a white-powdered face like a geisha's, and suffused with a sort of vivacious merriment like a naughty child.

Even Ines's white hair wasn't merely an older woman's *white hair*—it had been cut short and bristling like a rock star's punk hair and when you looked more closely, you saw that the "white" wasn't a soft white but a metallic white, obviously dyed.

And the gold sandals on Ines's tiny feet: three-inch heels that brought the flamboyant little woman to a precarious height of about five feet two. Her miniature toes peeped out, the nails polished ruby-red to match her fingernail polish and her pursed smiling lips.

"Please—come inside. And your suitcases—shall I . . ."

Though she'd been anticipating Ines's visit for several days, Mariana wasn't prepared for such a surprise: why hadn't Austin warned her that his former wife was disfigured? (Unless Austin didn't know? Was that possible? The missing eye had to mean cancer—didn't it?)

And there was Hortensa: plain, dour, with skinned-back hair and small close-set eyes, flat-heeled ballerina slippers, mud-colored polyester trousers and matching jacket, about Mariana's age and height but at least fifty pounds heavier. In her sullen face Mariana's bright smile was rudely deflected and in response to Mariana's greeting there came a barely audible mutter.

Mariana led their guests into the foyer. She was deeply embarrassed, anxious. She'd seen that Ines was amused by her discomfort over the missing eye. And whatever Ines was saying to Hortensa, in staccato Spanish, was probably not flattering to her, the *new, young wife.*

Mariana wanted to call for Austin to announce that their guests had arrived but she knew that Austin wouldn't like to be interrupted. In his bedroom, or in his bathroom, preparing to be seen by others, Austin did not care to be hurried in his elaborate personal grooming.

Mariana took the heavy tote bag from Hortensa and led the women into the guest wing of the house, which had windows facing the Pacific. All the while Ines was exclaiming, chattering brightly—Mariana couldn't follow her words, so heavily accented they might have been Spanish—while Hortensa followed in her aunt's wake, flat-footed and unsmiling.

You could see a family resemblance between the older woman and the younger: but where Ines's features were delicate, and the geisha-white cosmetic mask gave her a bizarre sort of histrionic beauty, Hortensa's features were coarsened and plain; in defiance of her aunt's glamour the niece wore no makeup on her sallow

skin, had done nothing to soften the effect of her coarse thick
eyebrows, and refused to stretch her thin, flat, colorless lips into
anything approaching a courteous smile.

Where the aunt was petite, a doll of a woman who couldn't
have weighed more than ninety pounds, the niece was hefty,
stolid as a young heifer; inside the mud-colored polyester jacket
her breasts were enormous as swollen, sagging fruit.

Mariana's first houseguests, in her new marriage! She was feeling just slightly faint, Ines's perfume like a rich, overripe fruit
wafted to her nostrils.

She hoped that Austin would hear Ines's high-pitched voice
or the sharp clatter of her shoes against the tile floor. Mariana
wanted to scream at him *Come here! Help me! Your wife has arrived.*

"Aus-tin! How good to see you! And not changed at all—or
almost. A year flies by quickly, does it?—so much happens, yet
no *change.*"

Whatever Ines was chattering in her maddening bright voice
Mariana couldn't follow. She saw that Austin greeted his former
wife with a forced sort of hearty enthusiasm, as he might have
greeted a visitor to the Institute whom he knew slightly; with a
stiff little smile he stooped to allow her to brush her lips against
both his cheeks, leaving a ruby smear on both cheeks that would
have annoyed him greatly if he'd known. For the evening Ines
had changed into a startling costume—a puckered strapless top
in deep purple satin, incongruous with her bony shoulders and
thin, flaccid upper arms, and a flimsy skirt like cobwebs, cut at

an angle so that it looked torn. Around her thin neck was a jade necklace that had to be, Mariana surmised, a gift from Austin, for it very much resembled the jade necklace Mariana herself was wearing, though it wasn't so ornate or so heavy as Mariana's. Ines's alarmingly bare shoulders gave her a fragile but dignified look. Inside the puckered satin, her breasts were small as if shrunken.

The shadowy socket where her right eye should have been gave her face a squinting asymmetrical cast like a female face in a Picasso painting. Yet you could see that Ines had been beautiful, once; and had retained the image of that beauty even now.

What a strange couple they were: the bristly-white-haired woman so short, and so petite; the former husband so much larger, looming over her. Ines did suddenly seem, despite her air of frantic gaiety, considerably older than Austin.

And Mariana saw that yes, Austin must have known about Ines's missing eye, for he showed no surprise, still less alarm or concern, at the ghastly sight of the empty socket; in fact he'd barely glanced at Ines's festive face, turning quickly to Hortensa, with a similarly hearty/impersonal greeting and a handshake.

Hortensa made no effort to appear friendly, or even very animated. Neither she nor Austin hugged the other or brushed lips against cheeks. Mariana was impressed with the sulky girl's resistance to Austin's charm. She thought *She is immune to the man and wants him to know.*

It was an old sour relationship, Mariana supposed. Austin and Hortensa were linked by marriage, or had once been—obscure relatives thrown together with nothing to say to each other.

Drinks? Would they like drinks? Briskly Austin ushered his guests into the living room, urging them to sit down on the long white-leather sofa facing the view of the city in the distance, the Bay and bridges. In fading sunlight the Golden Gate Bridge shimmered just barely visible.

"Ah! As always—*espectacular*! If there is no worry—shall I say this?—of *el terremoto*."

Ines remained on her feet speaking lightly, laughing. Mariana knew that *el terremoto* meant *the earthquake* and that this subject stirred in Austin, as in other longtime residents of the San Francisco/Berkeley area, a predictable sort of dismissive laughter.

"Well—it will take more than *el terremoto* to move me from here."

Mariana had the idea that this was an old issue. Many times, far too many times, *the wife* and *the husband* had spoken of it, and always *the husband* would make the same offhanded reply.

"Mariana, dear—what of you?"

"Yes? What?"

"Does *el terremoto* not frighten you, a little?"

Mariana tried to think. It was a fact, she'd given little thought to the possibility of an earthquake in this precarious hillside dwelling. As she'd given little thought to the possibility of a fire, a flash flood, landslide.

"Mariana is not an alarmist, Ines. She is a practical person—she knows to live *here, now*."

This was the first time anyone had ever spoken of Mariana as *practical*. And in the third person, in her hearing, as if she were a very young child or in some way incapacitated.

Perhaps it was a fact, Mariana accepted the possibility of an earthquake in this beautiful place as a feature of her marriage. She was so very grateful for the marriage, a mere earthquake could not dissuade her.

"I haven't thought of it, I guess . . . I . . ."

Mariana's voice trailed off lamely. How weak Ines and Hortensa must think she was, this new, young wife of Austin's!

When he'd joined them a few minutes before, Austin had greeted Mariana with a distracted sort of affection. All the while he'd been staring in Ines's direction without exactly looking at Ines, as one might look in the direction of a blinding light without daring to confront it head-on.

Now he glanced at Mariana with a sharp crease of a frown between his eyebrows, as if he had but a vague idea who this person was, and why she was in his living room with his exotic Spanish ex-wife.

Gracelessly Hortensa had lowered her weight onto the sofa, at an end from which the shimmering view wasn't visible. She hadn't troubled to wash her somewhat greasy face or to change for the evening apart from removing the polyester jacket: beneath, she was wearing a rumpled T-shirt, matte black, with a faded sparkly image—a human face of some kind, glaring eyes, wild hair—Beethoven?

While Austin prepared drinks Ines continued to walk about in her clattery high heels, exclaiming at things—old, familiar— new, *bonito*. It was impossible to tell—impossible for Mariana to tell—if the vivacious little woman was sincerely admiring, or subtly mocking; if, drawing her former husband's attention to a sculpted "demon" from Mexico, or a grimacing Cambodian mask, or the lacquered Japanese screen, she meant to remind him cruelly of their shared past, or to congratulate him on having retained some of the beauty of their shared past. She spent some time examining the orchids, the bonsai trees, the little lemon tree.

Mariana thought *She will pick one of the little lemons and put it in her pocket.*

But Ines just complimented Austin on his beautiful house — seemingly without irony. Then, recalling Mariana, the new wife, turning to Mariana with a warm smile, to include her as well.

Seeing the empty socket beneath the arched eyebrow, Mariana felt a wave of faintness again.

And the other eye, the remaining eye—bright as reflected glass, beautifully made up and all but winking at the new, young wife.

Mariana excused herself to get appetizers from the kitchen, which she'd prepared earlier. Expensive cheeses, Austin's favorites, had been set out to warm, from the refrigerator; there were Greek olives, cashews, small perfect grapes, and Austin's favorite rye-crisp crackers. How grateful Mariana was to escape Ines's presence for even so brief a period of time—the impulse came strong, to run outside, along the graveled drive to the road, and—away.

But I am his wife now, he loves me. I belong here.

She wasn't so sure of this. The wave of faintness rose in her again, confused with a powerful scent of overripe peaches and a meaty odor from the rich cassoulet Austin had begun preparing the previous evening, that was simmering at a low heat in a Dutch oven on the counter.

When Mariana returned with the tray of appetizers, Austin and their guests were seated at uncomfortable angles to each other—Ines on the white-leather sofa facing the plate-glass window, Austin in a chair exactly perpendicular to Ines, and Hortensa at the far end of the sofa. But no one was looking at anyone else, and no one seemed, for the moment, to have anything to say.

Even Ines was just slightly uncomfortable. She had a habit of stroking her bare arm slowly, sensuously; caressing herself, as if to comfort herself.

Her bare arms were thin, crepey. Mariana saw what appeared to be tiny black ants on her arms, which were, of course, moles.

Moles on the nape of Ines's neck. A mole on the underside of her jaw.

Smiling, Mariana served the appetizers. She was very warm: beginning to perspire. Of course she'd showered earlier that day but not since and she dreaded Austin glancing at her, as he'd done once, not long ago, startled by a smell of her skin perhaps, when she'd become unexpectedly warm, and he'd asked her—not cruelly, not maliciously, but just a little playfully, teasing—if she hadn't had time to shower that morning?—and she'd been deeply embarrassed and ashamed.

She saw that the expensive Brie was soft and runny—Austin would approve. For this difficult evening she'd dressed in new clothes: a blue pleated top, a white pleated skirt. Around her neck was the heavy Chinese jade medallion, a gift from Austin. Her hair had begun to recover some of its glossy thickness and her skin was less sallow than it had been; she'd darkened her lips with a plum-colored lipstick that seemed to illuminate her face, to suggest hope. But Austin seemed to take little notice. The rich, runny Brie he spread thickly onto a cracker, eating hungrily.

Though Austin had spoken casually of his former wife's visit he had dressed for the occasion: his shirt was fine Egyptian cotton in a pale orange color, worn open at the throat; his trousers were dove-gray linen, with a sharp crease. He'd shaved for the second time that day, for his beard was dark, and grew in heavily.

Mariana thought *He's still in love with her. That is his secret.*

Rapidly then Ines and Austin exchanged news of mutual friends, acquaintances, children?—Mariana could barely follow their murmured words, that had the air of coded messages.

"Austin! How is—?"

"He's good. And how is—?"

"Very good! I think."

"And how is—?"

"Not so good."

"No! When was this?"

"A few months ago."

"How old?"

"Not old. Sixty-seven."

"Sixty-seven! Not old at all."

Yet, the ex-wife and the ex-husband did not exactly look at each other. There was a grim willfulness in their remarks as if a force impersonal to both were driving through them, coercing them. Mariana understood that they were bound together not by this web of names but by the unspoken loss at the core of their relationship—the infant Raoul.

No bond between *the fourth wife* and *the husband* could ever be so deep, so intimate as this—Mariana knew.

Mariana moved closer to the lonely-seeming Hortensa. She'd thought it strange—though, in the anxiety of the moment, she'd scarcely had time to think—that Ines had airily introduced herself as *Ines Zambranco* but her niece as merely *Hortensa*, as one might introduce a young child, or a servant. Yet Hortensa was a cellist of some reputation, wasn't she?—Mariana was eager to engage her in conversation.

"Austin told me that you play cello?—what a beautiful instrument! I used to play double bass, and piano; I mean, I've had training—lessons—twelve years of lessons—though at the present time, I seem to have given up. . . ." A feeling of loss swept through Mariana, for a moment she thought she might begin to cry: her face would crinkle like an infant's, and tears would run from her eyes. But brightly she said: "I hope it won't be permanent—giving up. If I could play with someone, I'd be happy to accompany on the piano, or try. . . ."

There was a piano in Austin's work-studio in this house, a small Steinway at which Austin occasionally played; one of Austin's talents was for composing music, Mariana had learned, though he'd set aside composing in recent years. He'd offered to pay for music lessons for Mariana with an Institute instructor, but Mariana had demurred, for the time being—"I don't feel very 'musical' right now."

Where did Hortensa live? How frequently did she travel to Spain? How often did she see her aunt Ines? Where had she had musical training and where did she play the cello?—eager questions that provoked Hortensa to replies, terse but not rude; glancing at Mariana almost shyly, Hortensa volunteered that she'd studied cello at Julliard and at the Royal Conservatory of Music in Madrid, with the distinguished Vincent Martínez; that she lived most of the time in New York City, which was where her mother and stepfather owned a brownstone in the West Seventies; she played cello where and when she could, most recently with a chamber music group called . . . Mariana saw that the young woman's eyes were dark, close-set and beautiful, with a sort of wariness as in one who has too often been baited into responding openly to another and then been rebuked.

Impulsively Mariana said, "Maybe—we could play together? I mean—I could accompany you on the piano. . . ."

"I don't have my cello with me. You didn't see me bring my cello, did you."

Hortensa's reply was just slightly sarcastic. Mariana chose not to hear.

"Well, I mean—sometime, Hortensa! When you and Ines visit Austin again."

Mariana rose to pass the appetizers another time. She saw that her hands, chilled, were trembling slightly.

"Ah!—you have the *nazar* here, still. This is very wise, Austin!"

In the dining room, Ines inspected the blue-glass "eye" beside the arched doorway. Mariana held her breath for it seemed that Ines was lifting the *nazar* from its hook and might drop it.

Two glasses of Austin's favorite chardonnay in the living room had brought a feverish flush to Ines's face, discernible even through the thick white cosmetic mask. Seen from behind, the white-haired woman looked touchingly frail—her bare shoulders, prominent backbone—the upper arms like those of a malnourished child. Yet Mariana felt that of the four of them, including even Austin, Ines was the most strong-willed and forceful.

"You see—I am never without my *nazar*"—Ines lifted her thin arm, to show the company a linked-gold bracelet on her left wrist, to which was attached a coin-sized *nazar* of blue glass. "Though it is 'just superstition'—as Austin says—it would be very foolish to travel across the Atlantic Ocean without such a precaution. And I insist my dear niece wears a *nazar,* too."

Hortensa, with the air of a put-upon adolescent, dutifully lifted her fleshy arm to display the bracelet on her wrist.

Ines said reprovingly: "The evil eye is all around us and now in cyberspace, too. One cannot be too cautious."

"Yes! So true! And yet—one must *live*."

Austin helped Ines settle into her chair, and would have helped Hortensa except the dour young woman had already seated herself. And there was Mariana, fully capable of seating herself, even if Austin had taken notice of her.

Four places at the dining room table, two on each side. Austin and *the fourth wife* would face *the first wife* and Hortensa, inescapably.

But Mariana was thinking now, though Austin was ignoring her, Austin was only stiffly attentive to Ines, looking toward her rather than at her. In the living room he'd remained sitting perpendicular to her, like a figure in an Edward Hopper painting in the presence of, yet not *with,* other figures; his smile was fixed, forced.

"So beautiful, as always! For a man alone, Austin knows to surround himself with the most exquisite things."

Ines was referring to the dining room, with its dark-red walls, brass-framed mirrors, and lithographs by Klee, Chagall, and Picasso; gaily she leaned over the table to sniff at a vase of purple and yellow iris Mariana had cut in the garden beside the house.

It wouldn't occur to Mariana until later, nor did it seem to have occurred to the others, that Austin was no longer a *man alone.*

"Ah, these are—artificial? I think so."

Mariana said no, she'd cut the flowers herself.

"Long ago, there were very fragrant flowers growing around this house," Ines said, cocking her head at Mariana, squinting her single sparkling eye, "but each year I have visited there are fewer. These have no fragrance at all, and could pass for *artificial*." Ines gave the word a chic Spanish pronunciation.

Mariana glanced at Austin for support, or sympathy, but Austin didn't appear to be listening. Between his eyebrows was a sharp knife-crease.

The first course was a light, frothy, and creamy mushroom soup Austin had prepared. Ines praised the soup effusively— "Ah! *Perfecto.*"

For the evening, Austin's longtime housekeeper Ana was helping in the kitchen, but Austin preferred to serve dinner guests in person, as if he had no hired help at all. Of course, Mariana was enlisted to help him with the heavy cassoulet. It was an elaborate Spanish meal comprised of a variety of ingredients— duck, sausage, pork, pancetta, ham hocks, beans—and provided a subject for much conversation, drawing in even Hortensa. Brought to the table at the same time was a large wooden bowl filled by Mariana with salad greens, cherry tomatoes, fresh basil and parsley, and chopped figs, tossed with Austin's olive-oil-and-vinegar dressing—a beautiful salad. And there was yet another bottle of red wine to be opened and poured, with ceremony; so Austin was preoccupied, and Mariana began to feel less acutely self-conscious.

It was an exquisite dinner. Austin prided himself on his cooking, and took as much pains with food and drink as he did with his professional work.

Yet the cassoulet was very rich. After two small forkfuls, Mariana began to lose her appetite.

Ines, too, ate sparingly. But the vivacious little woman was practiced at pushing food around her plate, flattering her host into thinking that she was busily consuming his food and relishing it.

And Hortensa ate heartily—seconds, thirds heaped by Austin onto her plate.

During the meal, Ines chattered brightly about California— "Only just a memory to me now. But—a memory!"

Mariana saw Austin flinch at this seemingly casual remark.

"Those trees! Eucalyptus are very dangerous in a windstorm, Mariana—yet more, in a firestorm. I've seen them burst into flame—it's astonishing, like a—holocaust. You can never look at a eucalyptus tree in quite the same way again."

Mariana smiled, perplexed. Had Ines—and Austin—lived through a firestorm? Or was Ines simply talking, aimlessly?

"Austin sneers at superstition. But there is something to it— the logic of chance—things happen to us for a reason. In the old folk tales there are no natural deaths—spirits cause them. If you are stricken, fall down, and die, it's the place where you die that is responsible—an evil spirit must dwell there. My grandmother told me about a woman who was careless in a cemetery, and dropped an urn, and an evil spirit leapt out of it and into her . . ."

Hortensa laughed, suddenly. Ines turned to her with a look of startled scorn.

"*Sí*, you young people will laugh. Until it happens to *you*."

Conversation now reverted to less sensitive subjects—Berkeley and San Francisco restaurants, *tapas* bars, Spanish cuisine vs. other cuisines. Ines led, and Austin followed, though with less enthusiasm than he usually showed, talking of food; for food was one of Austin's passions, perhaps in this phase of his life a primary passion, along with wine. Mariana saw that Austin still did not look directly at Ines, if he could avoid it; as if he simply couldn't bear to see her—his once-gorgeous young wife now decades older and disfigured.

Politely Austin turned his attention to Hortensa, asking her questions about her "musical career"—until at last Hortensa said, sharply, with no effort at being civil to her host, "I don't have a musical career. I try to get gigs, and I try very hard. And mostly I fail. And in the meantime I teach—children. When I can get them. I've never had a *career*, I've barely had a *life*. I am a worker in music, a member of the *proletariat*."

Before Austin could reply, Ines intervened: "Hortensa exaggerates of course! But it is true, for all her talent she has had ill luck. Even as she scorns superstition she has had ill luck not deserved by one who has worked so hard, with so much heart—but that will change one day soon, I am confident."

Again Hortensa laughed. She made no effort to defend herself against her aunt's brittle optimism but scooped more cassoulet onto her plate.

Mariana felt a pang of sympathy for the young woman. *It's because she is not beautiful. She is a homely girl—there is no place for her even in music.*

But when Mariana tried to reestablish a sympathetic rapport with Hortensa, Hortensa coolly ignored her.

As if to say *Who are you? Somebody's wife? Nobody gives a damn about you.*

Numbly Mariana rose from the table. She would clear the dishes away—she would bring in the dessert, an elegant crème brûlée prepared by a famous Berkeley caterer.

Austin sat at his place unmoving, as if Mariana were his servant.

In the kitchen, Ana took the dishes from Mariana quickly, to rinse at the sink. She would have come into the dining room with Mariana to help clear the table but Mariana told her no, please—"Austin prefers that you stay here."

How sad she felt, how anxious, even before their guests' arrival her husband had seemed oblivious of her; not that he was angry at her in the way she so dreaded, but rather that he seemed to have forgotten her. *Yes—my wife. My new, young wife. Which one is she . . .*

Mariana didn't want to think that their marriage was so fragile, a husk of a marriage—entered into far too swiftly on both sides, as in a romantic Latin film. She didn't want to think that she was with this much older man only because the man loved her: claimed to adore her.

She was empty, scoured-out inside. Her life had collapsed with her parents' deaths, she had never fully recovered. She had no love in her for this husband, nor the hope of love.

She returned to the dining room. Candlelight fluttered against the three uplifted faces—of which one, missing an eye, was turned to her, with a sly smile of recognition.

As Mariana passed by Ines's chair the white-haired little woman seized her hand to tug her roughly down and whisper in her ear: "You are safe, Mariana! *He* will never know your secret."

Mariana had sought, in her husband's filing cabinets and drawers, photographs of the predecessor-wives. But either Austin had not kept careful records of his domestic past or, deliberately, he'd bowdlerized these records after his divorces.

Yet in the oldest album Mariana had found what must have been a photograph of Ines Zambranco, crumpled and torn: a beautiful pale-blond young woman in oversized dark glasses, laughing as she exhaled a plume of smoke. She was wearing what appeared to be a silk shawl draped about her slender shoulders, fallen open to reveal the tops of her creamy-smooth breasts. Whoever had taken the picture—very likely Austin himself—had clearly adored this woman, leaning close to her, swaying above her.

On the back was scribbled in pencil *Amalfi—Oct. 1982.*

The year before the death.

Deaths.

* * *

"Dear Mariana! It has been a deep pleasure to meet *you*."

There was a subtle, sly emphasis upon *you*. So that Mariana was given to know, as Ines smiled coquettishly at her, that Ines had much more enjoyed being in Mariana's presence than in Austin's.

Was this sincere? Was anything about the one-eyed little woman sincere? Mariana had never met anyone for whom she felt such a visceral repugnance and dread; yet, perversely, a fascination. She could imagine Ines Zambranco's ruined face painted by a great artist—Picasso for instance. The demonic strangeness beneath the *faux*-female smile would exert an irresistible appeal.

"Though it has seemed—tonight—that we have met you before—both Hortensa and I agree—in this household. You— or someone very like you. In years past."

Ines spoke lightly yet urgently. She was heedless of Mariana's look of offended surprise at her remark.

"We sense that you have had a great loss in your life—and that Austin has taken you up, as one of his 'projects.' He is not comfortable with strong women—only women missing a part of their souls. Once I was the man's wife also, before I understood this. As others have been—to their destruction."

Austin was in another part of the house. Mariana had accompanied their guests into the guest wing with the ostensible intention of checking, another time, the bathroom and its supply of large soft towels.

She'd known that it might be dangerous to be alone with *the first wife*—yet here she was.

Hortensa, too, had drawn away from them, taking refuge in her bedroom with the door closed behind her.

"I hope—I am not alarming you? There is much that must be told—swiftly. Before *he* intervenes—as always."

Dinner had prevailed for too long—nearly two hours. A kind of anxious lassitude had settled over the table. Mariana had had an unaccustomed several glasses of red wine and was feeling dazed, a dull headache starting behind her eyes. Yet no one had made a move to rise from the table until at last Austin said, with an air of forced apology, "Well! Some of us have an early day tomorrow . . ."

The party broke up immediately. Hortensa had been yawning without troubling to cover her mouth. Ines was looking tired, though she continued to smile her bright effervescent smile like one who knows herself on camera.

Eager to escape to his study, Austin had said good night to his guests. In the large glass-walled room overlooking a view of the Bay he would check e-mail and cell phone calls until midnight or later.

Mariana wondered if Austin would expect her to join him there, to confer with him about their guests; how he thought the difficult evening had gone, and what plans had he made, if any, for the next morning. Ines would expect to speak with him in private—wasn't that the point of the visit? But Mariana sensed that she wouldn't be welcome in Austin's study just then.

Her husband had had more than enough female companionship for the time being.

Ines was saying, conspiratorially: "I can feel the tension in this household, like the air before an electric storm. *It has always been here*. For Austin is not a sane man, essentially—you must know this by now. His madness, he can disguise as many men do, so the woman comes to doubt her own sanity."

Ines was gripping Mariana by the wrist. The little woman's talon-fingers, covered in rings, closed about Mariana's wrist.

Mariana tried to pull away, weakly.

"I—I don't think. . . . I have to leave now. . . ."

"You're very young! And he has chosen you not for your looks —which is very fortunate, Mariana, let me tell you—for the man has made some foolish blunders in the past, drawn to beauty."

Mariana stood as if hypnotized, unable to move. What was this terrible woman saying—that Mariana was *not beautiful*?

But she knew this, of course. Only she had not realized that others knew.

"Dear Mariana—you are a spiritual person, we can see. You are not 'skin deep.' Don't be suffocated by the man. You seem breathless—short of breath—like other women Austin has possessed. And don't think of having children with him—as a way of being less lonely. He will woo them from you, or worse."

"I—I have not thought of that. I . . ."

"When he kisses you, a man like that, you can taste the poison, yes? A little poison toad dwells within him. Next time you will notice, his saliva has a numbing effect—*anestésico*."

Mariana was too shocked to wrench away from the woman. A frantic blush rose into her face, which was already warm from too much wine at dinner.

"It is essential not to allow this man to persuade you into performing certain—how d'you call it—'love acts' with him. Though you are his wife, yet he does not approve, truly. For when he talks with his man friends they laugh together, they say crude, cruel things, no one is spared—despite wives, daughters— mothers—none of us seem to matter to them, the company of men, the *dog pack,* when they are together. Also, Austin is a man of extreme convention, a 'puritan,' and will not respect you."

Mariana's face was burning now. For Ines's warning came too late—already she had acquiesced to certain requests of her husband's, couched in pleading/chiding terms. *Mariana I love you so. I adore you. It will not hurt you . . . it would mean so much to me.*

"Hortensa, too, fell prey to him, when she was very young. At thirteen, my niece was not so plain-faced, and not so heavy. She accompanies me here each time to show him she has not been broken by *him.* He pretends not to remember, it is funny—yes?"

"I—I don't believe that, Ines. That is not—not likely. . . ."

"Why, because my niece is not beautiful now? When young, a girl does not have to be *beautiful* but only just *young*—ask your *perro*-husband."

Ines tugged at Mariana's wrist so that she could murmur in Mariana's ear: "A baby with such a man is—a folly. So young, when we were married, he didn't want to be a father—though Austin wasn't so very young, he was at least thirty; and I was two

53

years older. It's a crisis in the life of a man, when he becomes a father for the first time—he must cease being a child himself and this is wrenching for some men. I mean—it is truly a shock to them—'narcissists.' Austin has told you, I hope—our little son Raoul died of 'crib death'—a terrible surprise—'sudden infant death syndrome' it is named. But no one knows what causes it. They say—sleeping on the stomach might be responsible, when the baby is very young. I did not place this baby on his stomach but on his back. Yet, when I returned, the baby was lying on his stomach, and he was not breathing. And Austin was in the house. This house. It is not the same house exactly now for he has renovated those rooms—the baby's room is vanished now. Always he would claim that he was out of the house but the fact is, Austin was in the house. He pretends not to remember, but I remember. And our *au pair* would remember—she'd hiked down into the town, because Austin was not prepared just then to drive down. You see—an infant so young could not turn himself over. An infant must be older than he was, to roll from his back onto his stomach. Yet our little Raoul was 'sleeping' on his stomach. And he had stopped breathing. Though his little body was hot—burning with fever. His little face so *flushed*. I will never forget that heat."

Ines brushed at her face with her fingertips. Her single eye leaked tears that shone on her thin, powdered cheek.

Now that Ines was stricken with emotion, that seemed heart-rendingly genuine, Mariana was deeply moved, though uncertain what to do. She felt guilty, and ashamed, for having disliked this pathetic little woman since she'd first set eyes on her; still more unconscionably, she'd been jealous of her.

"Ines, I'm so very sorry. Austin had told me—something of this. But—"

"But not that he was in the house, and was the last person to see our baby son alive—I know he was."

"I—I don't know about that. . . ."

"He expelled me from his bed—from his life—soon after. He caused me to flee back home—to my family—I had a collapse, and was hospitalized for eight months. *He* will tell the story, it was my film career I chose, over our baby. Yet in fact it was his own career—he did not want to be 'encumbered'—not to take the child with him wherever he would go of course, but just to *think* of the child, and to *be* the father—it was too soon in his career."

Ines was shuddering with sobs. Her white-powdered geisha face had begun to melt in streaked rivulets of tears and mascara. Her puckered purple-satin top looked ludicrous on the wasted female body. Mariana tried to comfort her, though without touching her—(almost, Mariana was frightened of touching Ines)—but finally, so moved by pity for the older woman, Mariana took Ines in her arms, and held her.

So frail! So small! Ines felt light as a mannequin, a mere husk.

But this was deceptive: Ines wasn't really frail. In a harsh whisper she told Mariana of the "wild, wonderful dream" she'd had for years—"Even before our young son was taken from me, long ago. How I would give the cruel husband a potion, to render his evil harmless; how I would make a mixture of my own pills—barbiturates, and tranquilizers—which I would give to him in some way he would not know. Even as a young man Austin was susceptible to sinus infections—he took antibiotics often. I would fill the prescription for him, for the antibiotics. But I would substitute for them my own powerful pills. How would he know the difference?—he would not know. He takes many antibiotics, as Americans do—sometimes the prescription would be for one every few hours, day following day for as long as twelve days. And when he fell asleep, from my pills, I would need only to press a pillow against his face—little Raoul may have died in such a way, a pillow pressed over his face." Ines paused, breathing rapidly. She drew away from Mariana, just slightly: Mariana could see the tip of the woman's pink tongue, like a tiny serpent-tongue, between the smudged-ruby lips. "Then, I would remove all the pills of mine, that had been in Austin's possession, and flush them down the toilet. It would be believed that Austin had swallowed barbiturates deliberately, of his own volition. No one would know—he could not have known. The evidence would suggest he had been careless with medication, or had taken his own life. If there was an autopsy—who would know? And so many people close to him, he had injured, who would *care*?"

Mariana staggered from Ines, speechless. Was the woman joking? Could she be serious?

"I—I have to go now, Ines. I can't—can't talk to you any longer now. Good night!"

Mariana turned away but Ines clutched at her with thin, strong arms. The smell that wafted from her febrile little body was almost too much for Mariana.

"Ah, dear Mariana! You could be my own daughter—I am sent to warn you, you see. I did not have the courage for my wild dream when I was young. But you—you will fight for your life. I will remain with you—in spirit. I will not abandon you."

Fight for your life. But Mariana could just flee the marriage, if she wished.

Unless Austin wouldn't allow her to leave. There was that possibility.

In recent weeks their nights together had become as unpredictable as the days. Austin was affectionate, you could say sexually voracious, greedy; unless he was distant and distracted. More often lately, Austin didn't come to bed until late, by which time Mariana was asleep. (Or pretending to be asleep.) Usually he rose at 7 A.M. brisk and cheerful and quick to tell Mariana—"Stay in bed a while. You need your sleep. You're recovering."

That night, Mariana fell into a deep sleep almost immediately. When Austin came to bed, an hour or so later, she didn't wake fully, but was wakened at another time, much later, by a cry somewhere in the house. She sat up, frightened, and Austin told her sharply: "Stay in bed. I'll see what it is."

He was muttering to himself, agitated, frightened. In bed he wore a baggy T-shirt and cotton shorts that were often sweated-through and now he reached for a terry-cloth robe in his closet, to shrug into as he hurried from the room. Mariana was uncertain what was happening—a break-in? A fire? Then she remembered their houseguests.

Groggy from having been awakened so abruptly Mariana stood in the doorway of the bedroom, listening.

A female voice, or voices. Austin's voice. Though Austin had forbidden her to follow him Mariana made her way barefoot and cautious to the other end of the house where Austin appeared to be pleading with someone. Was a door locked? Was Ines locked in the bathroom? What was that faint wailing sound, that seemed to be coming from a distance?

Mariana dared to come up behind Austin and clutch at his arm.

"What is it? What has happened?"

"Go back to bed, Mariana. Please. This doesn't concern you."

"But—is Ines ill? Has she hurt herself? Where is Hortensa?"

"God damn it, Mariana! Do as I tell you. *Go back to bed.*"

Mariana returned to the bedroom but not to bed. She was too excited, anxious.

Has she tried to hurt herself? Kill herself? In Austin's house?

That is her revenge. . . .

It must have been a half hour later, when the commotion in the guest wing had subsided, that Mariana saw, at an angle, the bright lights of a vehicle arriving on the roadway outside. At first she thought it must be a medical vehicle but she didn't see a flashing light, had not heard a siren, but she could hear a dispatcher's radio voice.

Shortly then Mariana saw figures on the front walk, not clearly but at an angle. She had to bring her face close to the window, to see slantwise what was going on. A tall figure—this would be Austin—was walking with another tall figure—Hortensa?—and between them was a child-sized individual, limp-limbed, who had to be Ines. Mariana cranked open a window to hear the frail pettish familiar voice—"I am not crippled for Christ's sake. I can walk as well as any of you—God damn you!" The driver of the vehicle, evidently a taxi, took luggage from Austin and placed it in the trunk. After some difficulty, Ines was bundled into the backseat with Hortensa. Austin slammed the door and conferred with the driver, and the women were borne away in the chill mist of a dawn in the Berkeley hills.

Mariana examined the guest bathroom in which Ines had locked herself. Both the sink and the Mexican tile floor were damp; the sink had a faint-red hue that made Mariana feel sick to see.

In the wastebasket were blood-soaked tissues. Not just a few but a dozen. *She cut herself. She bled, in this house. We will never be free of her now.*

Austin came to look for Mariana, pulled her out of the airless bathroom and slammed the door. He was flushed with emotion, his hair disheveled and his jaws unshaven. Mariana asked what had happened and Austin said it was none of her concern and Mariana said of course it was her concern: she was his wife, she lived in this house, too. Had Ines tried to hurt herself? Had she cut herself? With a razor? *What had happened?*

Austin said, with a pose of indifference: "She's gone. And she won't be back. That's all you need to know."

Mariana followed him into the other part of the house. She saw that he was stroking his unshaven jaws with a look of chagrin and rage. But the rage wasn't for her, at least. She said: "She's not well. She's been wounded by—someone. Why didn't you warn me that she was missing an eye? It was such a shock to open the door and see her, without being prepared."

"Missing—what?"

"Missing an eye. Her right eye, I think. Why didn't you warn me?"

Austin stared at Mariana as if he suspected she was trying to joke with him, at this inopportune time. He took hold of her arm at the elbow, to give her a little shake, as one might give a willful child.

"Missing an eye? What on earth are you talking about now, Mariana?"

"Her eye. Ines's right eye. The empty socket—it's so horrible to see, and so sad. . . ."

"You've had too much to drink. You *can't drink,* Mariana. You know that."

"Her eye—her eye is missing. She must have had cancer. The poor woman, how can she bear to look at herself in the mirror—how can she have a professional career—why doesn't she get outfitted with an artificial eye? It's so horrible to see, I'll have nightmares seeing that empty socket, it would have been kind of you to have warned me, Austin. . . ."

"Ines is not missing an eye. Ines has not had cancer—so far as I know. You're exhausted, and you're not being coherent. You haven't been any help in this crisis, you've made things worse with your hysteria. All you need to know, Mariana, is that Ines will never visit this house again. You will never see that woman again—don't worry."

With grave disappointment Austin spoke. As Mariana stared after him he walked off, heavy-footed, disgusted.

In the days and weeks following *the first wife's* visit Mariana was susceptible to headaches, indigestion, insomnia.

Mariana was keenly aware of how the house, Austin's beautiful house, had been altered.

It was not simply the husband's wariness in her company: his air of caution, though often he smiled at her and seemed to agree with her, as one might humor a deranged person; it was something more fundamental, a *distrust* of her, as of a stranger living in his household.

She fell into a habit of touching her eye: the left eye.

She fell into a habit of touching her eye: the right eye. To assure herself that it was there, and not merely a socket.

She fell into the habit of stroking her bare arm slowly and sensuously, as if comforting herself. Her fingertips seeking out tiny near-invisible moles in the pale skin.

It was clear, the atmosphere of the house had been altered. The quality of the light refracted from the Bay miles away, as if a minuscule drop of toxin had been introduced.

The most gorgeous orchid plant, a faint rosy pink striated with dark stripes, began to drop its petals.

Nothing Mariana could do seemed to help. One by one the petals fell until only ugly skeletal stick-stalks remained.

Glossy leaves from the jade plant began to fall. If Mariana watered the plant, leaves fell; if Mariana held back from watering the plant, leaves fell.

One of the bonsai trees began to wither.

Mariana was in a panic wondering if she should hurry out to a florist's shop and buy new, healthy plants. For Austin would blame her, she knew. It had fallen to her to oversee the plants.

Probably, it was too late. He'd noticed the sickly orchids, in particular. If Mariana tried to deceive him, that would not go well with her.

A crack appeared in one of the beautiful earthen-colored Catalan bowls, but Mariana was certain she had not touched for months.

She examined the blue-glass *nazar* hanging by the doorway. Waiting for it to slip from her fingers and shatter on the floor— but it did not, yet.

What a hell, insomnia! The raging fever returned to her, after nearly a year.

Long ago Mariana had used up the barbiturates her mother's doctor had prescribed for her back in Connecticut. She made an appointment in Berkeley, without Austin's knowledge, and received a prescription for sleeping pills. She'd told the doctor that she and her husband would be traveling to Europe soon, and that she needed as many pills as he could give her. She filled the prescription at once, at the nearest pharmacy. Driving home along the narrow twisting hillside roads she felt a terrible dryness in her mouth, as if she'd already begun taking barbiturates and would never again be fully awake. Home in the house she was grateful to be alone—so grateful! Austin was at the Institute and would return home late. He, too, had had difficulty sleeping in recent weeks, his sinus headaches had returned since Ines's visit and he was beginning a strict regimen of antibiotics.

In the living room flooded with late-afternoon light from the sky above the Pacific, Mariana spread a half-dozen of the gleaming little pearl-pills on the palm of her hand, staring at them with a faint, fading smile as if trying to recall their meaning.

SO NEAR   ANY TIME   ALWAYS

Oh! he was smiling at me.

Was he smiling—at *me*?

Quick then looking away, looking down at my notebook—where I'd been taking notes for a science-history paper—while spread about me on the highly polished table were opened volumes of *Encyclopedia Britannica, World Book of Science, Science History Digest.*

A hot blush rose into my face. I could not bring myself to glance up, to see the boy at a nearby table, similarly surrounded by spread-open books, staring at me.

Though now I was aware of him. Of his quizzical-friendly stare.

Thinking *I will not look up. He's just teasing.*

In 1977: still an era of libraries.

In the suburban branch library that had been a millionaire's mansion in the nineteenth century. In the high-ceilinged reference room. Shelves of books, gilt-glinting titles, brilliant sunshine through the great octagonal window so positioned in the wall that, seated at one of the reference tables, you could see only the sky through the inset glass-panes like an opened fan.

Will not look up yet my eyes lifted involuntarily.

Still he was smiling at me. A stranger: a few years older than I was.

Never smile or speak to strange men but this was a boy not a man.

I wondered if he was a student at St. Francis de Sales Academy for Boys, a private Catholic school where tuition was said to be as high as college tuition and where the boys, unlike boys at my school, had to wear white shirts, ties, and jackets to class.

Smiling at me in a way that was so tender, so kindly, so *familiar*.

As if, though I didn't know him, he knew me. As if, though I didn't know him, yet somehow I did know him, but had forgotten as you feel the tug of a lost dream, unable to retrieve it, yet yearning to retrieve it, like groping in darkness, in a room that should be familiar to you.

He knows me! He understands.

I was sixteen. I was a high school junior. I was *young for my age* it was said—(not to me, directly)—which translated into an adult notion of *underdeveloped sexuality, emotional immaturity, childishness.*

It wasn't so unusual that a boy might smile at me, or a man might smile at me, if I was alone. A young girl alone will always attract a certain kind of quick appraising (male) attention.

If whoever it was hadn't seen my face clearly, or my skin.

Seen from a little distance, I looked like any girl. Or almost.

Seen from the front, I looked like a girl of whom relatives say
Her best feature is her smile!

Or, *If only she would smile just a little more—she'd be pretty.*

Which wasn't true, but well meaning. So I tried not to absolutely hate the relative who said it.

This boy was no one I'd ever encountered before, I was sure.
If I had, I would have remembered him.

He was very handsome, I thought. Though I scarcely dared
to look at him.

Mostly I was conscious of his round, gold-rimmed glasses
that gave him a dignified appearance. Inside the lenses his eyes
were just perceptibly magnified, which gave them a look of
blurred tenderness.

His face was angular and sharp-boned and his hair was scru-
pulously trimmed with a precise part on one side of his head,
the way men wore their hair years ago; unlike most guys his age,
anyway most guys you'd see in Strykersville, he was wearing an
actual shirt not a T-shirt—a short-sleeved shirt that looked like
it might be expensive.

Smiling at me in this tentative way to signal that if I was
wary of him, or frightened of him, it was OK—it was cool. He
wouldn't bother me further.

He'd been taking notes in a notebook, too. Now he returned to his work, studious and intense as if he'd forgotten
me. I saw that he was left-handed—leaning over the library
table with his left arm crooked at the elbow so he could write
with that hand.

A curious thing: he'd removed his wristwatch to position it on the tabletop so that he could see the time at a glance. As if his time in the library might be precious and limited and he feared it spilling out into the diffuse atmosphere of the public library in which, like sea creatures washed ashore, eccentric-looking individuals, virtually always male, seemed drawn to pursue obsessive reference projects.

So I continued with my diligent note-taking. *Amphibian ancestors. Evolution. Prehistoric amphibians: why gigantic? Present-day amphibians: why dwindling in numbers?*

Trying not to appear self-conscious. With this unknown boy fewer than fifteen feet away facing me as in a mirror.

A hot blush in my cheeks. And I regretted having bicycled to the library without taking time to fasten my hair back into a ponytail so now it was straggly and windblown.

My hair was fair-brown with a kinky little wave. Very like the boy's hair except his was trimmed so short.

A strange coincidence! I wondered if there were others.

My note-taking was scrupulous. If the boy glanced up, he would see how serious I was.

. . . environmental emergency, fate of small amphibians worldwide . . .

. . . exact causes unknown but scientists suggest . . .

. . . radical changes in climate, environment . . . invasive organisms like fungi . . .

Then, abruptly—this was disappointing!—after fewer than ten minutes the boy with the gold-rimmed glasses decided to leave:

got to his feet—tall, lanky, stork-like—slipped his wristwatch over his bony knuckles, briskly shut up the reference books and returned them to the shelves, hauled up a heavy-looking backpack, and without a glance in my direction exited the room. The soles of his sneakers squeaked against the polished floor.

There I remained, left behind. Accumulating notes on the tragically endangered class of creatures Amphibia, for my earth science class.

Did it occur to you to exit the library at the rear? Just in case he was waiting at the front.

Did it occur to you it might be a good idea not to meet up with this boy?

Of course it didn't occur to you, he might be older than he appeared.

He might be other than he appeared.

Of course it didn't occur to you and why?

Because you were sixteen. An immature sixteen.

A not-pretty girl. A lonely girl.

A desperate girl.

"Hey. Hi."

He was waiting for me outside the library.

This was such a shock to me, a relief and a wonder—as if nothing so extraordinary had ever happened, and could not have been predicted.

I had assumed that he'd left. He'd lost interest in me and he'd left and I would not see him again as sometimes—how often, I didn't care to know—male interest in me, stimulated initially, mysteriously melted, evaporated, and vanished.

But there he was waiting for me, in no way that might intimidate me: just sitting on the stone bench at the foot of the steps, leafing through a library book he was about to slide into his backpack.

Seeing the look of surprise in my face the boy said "hi!" a second time, smiling so deeply, tiny knife-cuts of dimples appeared in his lean cheeks.

Shyly I said hello. My heart was beating in a feathery-light way that made it hard for me to breathe.

And shyly we stared at each other. To be *singled out* was such an unnerving experience for me, I had no idea how to behave.

To feel this sensation of unease and excitement, and so quickly.

Like a basketball tossed at me without warning, or a hockey puck skittering along the playing field in the direction of my feet—I had to react without thinking or risk getting hurt.

Boldly, yet not aggressively he asked my name. And when I told him he repeated "Lizbeth" and told me his name—"Desmond Parrish."

Amazingly, he held out his hand for me to shake—as if we were adults.

He'd gotten to his feet, in a chivalrous gesture. He was smiling so hard now, his glittery-gold glasses seemed to have become dislodged and he had to push them against the bridge of his nose with the flat of his hand.

"I wondered how long you'd stay in there. I was hoping you wouldn't stay until the library closed."

SO NEAR ANY TIME ALWAYS

Awkwardly I murmured that I was doing research for a paper in my earth science class. . . .

"Earth science! Quick tell me: what's the age of the Earth?"

"I—I don't remember. . . ."

"Multiple-choice question: The age of Earth is (a) fifty million years (b) three hundred sixty thousand years (c) ten thousand years (d) forty billion years (e) four point five billion years. No hurry!"

Trying to remember, and to reason: but he was laughing at me.

Teasing-laughing. In a way to make my face burn with pleasure.

"Well, I know it can't be ten thousand years. So we can eliminate that."

"You're certain? Ten thousand years would be appropriate if Noah and his ark are factored in. You don't believe in Noah and his ark?"

"N-No . . ."

"How'd the animals survive the flood, then? Birds, human beings? Fish, you can see how fish would survive, no problem factoring in fish, but—mammals? Non-arboreal primates? How'd they manage?"

It was like trying to juggle a half-dozen balls at once, trying to talk to this very funny boy. Seeing that I was becoming flustered he relented, saying: "If you consider that life of some kind has been around about three point five billion years, then it figures, right?—the answer is (e) four point five billion years. That's a loooong time, before October ninth, 1977, in Strykersville, New York. A looong time before *Lizabeth* and *Desmond.*"

71

Like a TV stand-up comic Desmond Parrish spoke rapidly and precisely and made wild-funny gestures with his hands.

No one had ever made me laugh so hard, so quickly. So breathlessly.

As if it was the most natural thing in the world Desmond walked with me to the street. He was a head taller than me—at least five feet eleven. He'd swung his heavy backpack onto his shoulders and walked with a slight stoop. Covertly I glanced about to see if anyone was watching us—anyone who knew me: *Is that Lizbeth Marsh? Who on earth is that tall boy she's with?*

It seemed natural, too, that Desmond would walk me to my bicycle, leaning against the wrought iron fence. Theft was so rare in Strykersville in those years, no one bothered with locks.

Desmond stroked the chrome handlebars of my bicycle, that were lightly flecked with rust—the bicycle was an English racer, but inexpensive, with only three gears—and said he'd seen me bicycling on the very afternoon he and his family had moved to Strykersville, twelve days before: "At least, I think she was you."

This was a strange thing to say, I thought. As if Desmond really did know me, and we weren't strangers.

Somehow it happened, Desmond and I were walking together on Main Street. I wasn't riding my bicycle, Desmond was pushing it, while I walked beside him. His eyes were almond-shaped and fixed on me in a way both tender and intense, that made me feel weak.

Already the feeling between us was so vivid and clear—*As if we'd known each other a long time ago.*

People scorn such an idea. People laugh, who know no better.

"Lizbeth, you can call me 'Des.' That's what my friends call me."

Desmond paused, staring down at me with his strange wistful smile.

"Of course, I don't have any friends in Strykersville yet. Just you."

This was so flattering! I laughed, to suggest that, if he was joking, I knew he'd meant to be funny.

"But I don't think that I will call you 'Liz'—'Lizbeth' is preferable. 'Liz' is plebian, 'Lizbeth' patrician. *You* are my patrician friend in plebian western New York State."

Desmond asked me where I lived, and where I went to school; he described himself as "dangling, like a misplaced modifier, between academic accommodations" in a droll way to make me smile though I had no idea what this meant.

At each street corner I was thinking that Desmond would pause and say good-bye; or I would summon up the courage to interrupt his entertaining speech and explain that I had to bicycle home soon, my parents were expecting me.

On Main Street we were passing store windows. Pedestrians parted for us, glancing at us with no particular interest as if we were a couple—*Lizbeth, Desmond.*

Desmond's arm brushed against mine by accident. The hairs on my arm stirred.

I saw a cluster of small freckles on his forearm. I felt a sensation like warmth lifting from his skin, communicated to me on the side of my body closest to him.

Though I was sixteen I had not had a boyfriend, exactly. Not yet.

I had not been kissed. Not exactly.

There were boys in my class who'd asked me to parties, even back in middle school. But no one had ever picked me up at home, we'd just met at the party. Often the boy would drift off during the course of the evening, with his friends. Or I'd have drifted off eager to summon my father to come pick me up.

Mostly I'd been with other girls, in gatherings with boys. We weren't what you would call a popular crowd and no one had ever *singled me out*. No one had ever looked at me as Desmond Parrish was looking at me.

Walking along Main Street! Saturday afternoon in October! So often I'd seen girls walking with their boyfriends, holding hands; I'd felt a pang of envy, that such a thing would never happen to *me.*

Desmond and I weren't holding hands of course. Not yet.

Beside us in store windows our reflections moved ghostly and fleeting—tall lanky Desmond Parrish with his close-trimmed hair and schoolboy glasses; and me, Lizbeth, beside him, closer to the store windows so that it looked as if Desmond were looming above me, protecting me.

At the corner of Main Street and Glenville Avenue, which would have been a natural time for me to take my bicycle from Desmond and bicycle home, Desmond suggested that we stop for a Coke, or ice cream—"If this was Italy, where there are *gelato* shops every five hundred feet, we'd have our pick of terrific flavors."

I'd never been to Italy, and would have thought that *gelato* meant Jell-O.

In the vicinity there was only the Sweet Shoppe, a quaint little ice cream–candy store of another era, which Desmond declared had "character"—"atmosphere." We sat at a booth beside a wall of dingy mirrors and each of us had a double scoop of pistachio-buttercrunch—this was Desmond's choice, which he ordered for me as well and paid for, in a generous, careless gesture, with a ten-dollar bill tossed onto the table for the waitress: "Keep the change for yourself, please."

The waitress, not much older than I was, could not have been more surprised than if Desmond had tossed a fifty-dollar bill at her.

In the Sweet Shoppe, tips were rare.

For the next forty minutes, Desmond did most of the talking. Sitting across from me in the booth he leaned forward, elbows on the sticky tabletop, his shoulders stooped and the tendons in his neck taut. By this time I was beginning to feel dazed, hypnotized—I had not ever been made to feel so *significant* in anyone's eyes.

Kindly and intense in his questioning Desmond asked me more about myself. Had my family always lived in Strykersville, what did my father do, what were my favorite subjects at school, even my favorite teachers—though the names of Strykersville High School teachers could have meant nothing to him. He asked me my birth date and seemed surprised when I told him (April 11, 1961)—"You look younger"—and possibly for a moment this was disappointing to him; but then he smiled his quick dimpled smile as if he were forgiving me, or finding a way he could accept my age, "—you could be, like, thirteen."

This was so. But I had never thought of it as an advantage of any kind.

"Life becomes complicated when living things 'mature'—the apparatus of a physical body is, essentially, to bring forth another physical body. If that isn't your wish, 'maturity' is a pain in the ass."

I laughed, to show Desmond that I knew what he meant. Or, I thought I knew what he meant.

Though I wasn't sure why it was funny.

I said, "My mother tells me not to worry—I'll grow when I'm 'ready.'"

"When your genes are 'ready,' Lizbeth. But they may have their own inscrutable plans."

Desmond told me that his family was descended from "lapsed WASP" ancestors in Marblehead, Massachusetts; he'd been born in Newton and went to grade school there; then he'd been sent to a "posh, Englishy-faggoty" private school in Brigham, Massachusetts—"D'you know where Brigham is? In the heart of the Miskatonic Valley." Yet it also seemed that his family had spent time living abroad—Scotland, Germany, Austria. His father—"Dr. Parrish"—(Desmond pronounced "Dok-tor Parrish" in a way to signal how pompous he thought such titles were)—had helped to establish European research institutes connected to a "global" pharmaceutical company—"The name of which I am forbidden to reveal, for reasons also not to be revealed."

Desmond was joking, but serious, too. Pressing his forefinger against his pursed lips as if to swear me to secrecy.

When we parted finally in the late afternoon, Desmond said he hoped we would see each other again soon.

Yes, I said. I would like that.

"We could walk, hike, bicycle—read together—I mean, read aloud to each other. We don't always have to *talk*."

Desmond asked me my telephone number and my address but didn't write the information down—"It's indelibly imprinted in my memory, Lizbeth. You'll see!"

I have a boyfriend!

My first boyfriend!

A passport, this seemed to me. To a new wonderful country only glimpsed in the distance until now.

He hated the telephone, he said: "'Talking blind' makes me feel like I've lost one of my senses."

He preferred just showing up, after school, at my house.

For instance, on the day after we'd first met, he bicycled to my house without calling first, and we spent two hours talking together on the rear, redwood deck of my house. So casually he'd turned up, on a new-model Italian bicycle with numerous speeds, his head encased in a shiny yellow helmet—"Hey, Lizbeth; remember me?"

My mother was stunned. My mother, to whom I hadn't said a word about meeting Desmond the previous day, for fear that I would never see him again—clearly astonished that her plain-faced and immature younger daughter had a visitor like Desmond Parrish.

When my mother came outside onto the deck to meet him, Desmond stood hastily, lanky and tall and "adult": "Mrs. Marsh, it's wonderful to meet you! Lizbeth has told me such intriguing things about you."

"'Intriguing'? Me? She has? Whatever—?"

It was comical—(cruelly, I thought it was comical)—that my mother hadn't a clue that Desmond was joking; that even the gallant way in which he shook my mother's hand, another surprise to her, was one of his sly jokes.

But Desmond was sweet, funny, *affectionate*—as if the adult woman he was teasing on this occasion, and would tease on other occasions, was a relative of his: his own mother perhaps.

"D'you believe in serendipity, Mrs. Marsh? A theory of the universe in which nothing is an accident—nothing *accidental*. Our meeting here, and the three of us here together, 2:24 P.M., October 10, 1977, was destined to occur from the start of time, the Big Bang that set all things in motion. Which is why it feels so right."

Charmed by her daughter's new friend, like no other friend Lizbeth had ever brought home, female or male, my mother pulled up a deck chair and sat with us for a while; clearly she was impressed with Desmond Parrish when he mentioned to her, as if by chance, that his father was a "research scientist"—with an "MD from Johns Hopkins"—the new district supervisor of a "global" pharmaceutical company with a branch in Rochester, a forty-minute commute from Strykersville.

Immediately my mother said: "In Rochester? Nord Pharmaceuticals?"

Desmond seemed reluctant to admit a connection with the gigantic corporation that had been in the news intermittently in the past several years, as he seemed reluctant to tell my mother specifically where his family had moved in Strykersville, in fact not in the city but in a suburban-rural gated community north of the city called Sylvan Hills.

"It must be beautiful there. I've seen some of the houses from the outside. . . ."

"That might be the best perspective, Mrs. Marsh. From the outside."

My mother was a lovely woman of whom it would never be said that she was in any way socially ambitious, or even socially conscious; yet I saw how her eyes moved over Desmond Parrish, noting his neatly brushed hair, his clean-shaven lean jaws and polished eyeglasses, his fresh-laundered sport shirt with the tiny crocodile on the pocket; noting the handsome wristwatch with the large, elaborate face—(Desmond had shown me how the watch not only told time but also told the temperature, the date, the tides, the barometric pressure, and could be used as a compass)—and his close-clipped, clean nails.

"You should come to dinner soon, Desmond! It would be nice to meet your parents sometime, too."

"Yes. You're right, Mrs. Marsh. It would be."

Desmond spoke politely, just slightly stiffly. I sensed his rebuff of my mother's spontaneous invitation but my mother didn't seem to notice.

He'd brought with him, in his backpack, a Polaroid camera with which he took several pictures of me, when we were alone again. As he snapped the pictures he was very quiet, squinting at me through the viewfinder. Only once or twice he spoke—"Don't move! Please. And look at me with your eyes—fully. Straight to the heart."

I was very self-conscious about having my picture taken. Badly I wanted to lift my hands, to hide my face.

Nearby on the deck lay our golden retriever Rollo, an older dog with dun-colored hair and drowsy eyes; he'd regarded Desmond with curiosity at first, then dropped off to sleep; now, when Desmond began taking my picture, he stirred, moved his tail cautiously, came forward, and settled his heavy head in Desmond's lap in an unexpected display of trust. Desmond petted his head and stroked his ears, looking as if he were deeply moved.

"Rollo! 'Rollo May' is enshrined in my DNA. This is why fate directed me to Strykersville, Lizbeth. From the Big Bang— onward—to *you*."

We hiked in Fort Huron Park. We bicycled along a towpath beside the lake. And there was a boat rental, rowboats and canoes, and impulsively I said, "Let's rent a rowboat, Des! Please."

The lake was called Little Huron Lake. Long ago my father had taken Kristine and me out in a rowboat here and the memory was still vivid, thrilling. But I had not been back in years and was surprised to see how relatively few boats there were in the rental.

Desmond spoke slowly, thoughtfully. As if an idea, like a Polaroid print, were taking shape in his mind.

"Not a rowboat, Lizbeth—a canoe. Rowboats are crude. Canoes are so much more—responsive."

Desmond took my hand as an adult might take a child's hand and walked with me to the boat rental. It was the first time he'd taken my hand in this way, in a public place—his fingers were strong and firm, closed about mine. With a giddy sensation I thought *This is life! This is how it is lived.*

There was a young couple in one of the canoes, the girl at the prow and the man at the stern wielding the paddle. The girl's red-brown hair shone in the sun. As the canoe rocked in the waves the girl gave a frightened little cry though you could see that there was little danger of the canoe capsizing.

"I'm afraid of canoes, I think. I've never been out in one."

"Never been in a canoe!"

Desmond laughed, a high-pitched sort of laugh, excited, perhaps a little anxious. Clearly, this was an adventure for him, too. Squatting on the small dock he inspected each of the canoes, peering into it, stroking the sides as a blind man might have touched it, to determine its sturdiness. At least, that's what I thought he must be doing.

"The Indians made canoes of wood, of course. Beautifully structured, shaped vessels. Some were small, for just two people —like these. Some were long, as long as twenty feet—for war."

The boat-rental man came by, a stocky bearded man, and said something to Desmond that I didn't quite hear, which seemed to upset Desmond who reacted abruptly, and oddly—he stood, returned to me and grabbed my hand and again hauled me forward, this time away from the boat rental.

"Some other time. This is not the right time."

"What did the man say to you? Is something wrong?"

"He said—'Not the right time.'"

Desmond appeared shaken. His face was ashen, grave. His lips were downturned and twitching.

I could not believe that the boat-rental person had actually said to Desmond "Not the right time"—but I knew that if I questioned Desmond I would not find out anything more.

"If I died, it would be just temporary. Until a new being was born."

"That's reincarnation?"

"Yes! Because we are immortal in spirit, though our bodies may crumble to dust."

Desmond removed his gold-rimmed glasses to gaze at me. His eyes were large, liquidy, myopic. There was a tenderness in his face when he spoke in such a way that made me feel faint with love for him—though I never knew if he was speaking sincerely or ironically.

"I thought you were a skeptic—you've said. Isn't reincarnation unscientific? In our earth science class our teacher said—"

"For God's sake, Lizbeth! Your science teacher is a secondary-public-school teacher in Strykersville, New York! Say no more."

"But, if there's reincarnation," still I persisted, for it seemed crucial to know, "—where are all the extra 'souls' coming from? Earth's population is much larger than it ever was in the past, especially thousands of years ago. . . ."

Desmond dismissed my objection with an airy wave of his hand.

"Reincarnation is *de facto,* whether you have the intellectual apparatus to comprehend it. We are never born entirely 'new'— we inherit our ancestors' genes. That's why some of us, when we meet for the first time, it isn't the first time—we've known each other in a past lifetime."

Could this be true? I wanted to think so.

As Desmond spoke, more and more I was coming to think so.

"We can recognize a 'soul mate' at first sight. Because of course the 'soul mate' has been our closest friend from that other lifetime even if we can't clearly remember."

Desmond had taken out his Polaroid and insisted upon posing me against a backdrop of flaming sumac, in a remote corner of Fort Huron Park where we'd bicycled on a mild October Saturday.

Each time Desmond and I were together, Desmond took pictures. Some of these he gave to me, as "mementos"—most, he kept for himself.

"A picture is a memento of a time already past—passing into oblivion. That's why some people don't smile when they're photographed."

"Is that why you don't smile?"

"Yes. A smiling photograph is a joke, when it's posthumous."

"Posthumous—how?"

"Like, above an obituary."

It was so, when I tried to take Desmond's picture with my little Kodak camera, he refused to smile. After the first attempt, he hid his face behind outstretched fingers—"*Basta.* Photographers hate to be photographed, that's a fact."

Another time he said, mysteriously, "There are crude images of me in the public world, for which I had not given permission. If you take a picture, someone might appropriate it, and make a copy—you're using film. Which is why I prefer the Polaroid, that is unique and one time only."

When Desmond photographed me, he "posed" me—gripping my shoulders firmly, positioning me "in place." Often he turned my head, slightly—his long fingers framing my face with a grip that would have been strong if I'd resisted but was gentle since I complied.

More than once, Desmond asked me about my family—my "ancestors."

I told him what I knew. I'd wondered if he was teasing me.

Several times I told him that I had just a single, older sibling—my sister Kristine. Either Desmond seemed to forget this negligible fact, or he had a preoccupation with the subject of siblings.

He was curious about Kristine—he wanted to "see" her—(at a distance)—"Not necessarily meet her." And just once did Desmond meet Kristine, by accident when he and I were walking our bicycles across a pedestrian bridge, in the direction of Fort Huron Park and Kristine, with two of her friends, was approaching us.

Kristine was twenty years old at this time, a student at Wells College home for the weekend.

"Kristine! I've heard such great things about you," Desmond said, shaking my sister's hand vigorously, "—Lizbeth talks about you all the time."

This remark, which had so charmed my mother, fell flat with Kristine who stared at Desmond with something like alarm. "Yes? I'll bet."

Kristine spoke coolly. Her smile was forced and fleeting. She made no attempt to introduce Desmond to her friends—(girls she'd known in high school)—who also stared at Desmond who loomed tall and lanky and ill-at-ease smiling awkwardly at them.

I was furious with Kristine and her friends: their rudeness.

They're jealous of me. That I have a boyfriend.

They don't want me to be happy, they want me to be like them.

Afterward, Desmond asked about Kristine: was she always so *hostile*?

"Yes. I mean—no! Not always."

"She didn't seem to like me."

Desmond spoke wistfully. Yet I sensed incredulity, even anger beneath.

I said, "We get along better now that she's away at college, but it used to be hard—hard on me—to be her younger sister. Kristine is so critical, bossy—sarcastic. . . . Always thinks she knows what's best for me . . ."

Maybe this wasn't altogether true. My older sister was genuinely fond of me, too, and would be hurt to hear these words. My face smarted with embarrassment, that Kristine hadn't been nearly so impressed with Desmond as I'd hoped, or as Desmond might have hoped.

She had to be jealous! That was it.

Desmond said, "She looked at me as if—as if she 'knew' me. But she doesn't 'know' me. Not at all."

Later he said, "I'm an only child. Which is why I'm fated to be an outsider, a loner. Which is why my favorite writer has always been Henry David Thoreau—'The greater part of what my neighbors believe to be good I believe in my heart to be bad.'"

At home, Kristine said: "This Desmond Parrish. Mom was telling me about him and he isn't at all what Mom said, or you've been saying—it's all *an act*. Can't you see it?"

"An act—how? What do you mean?"

"I don't know. There's something not right about him."

"'Not right'—how? He's a wonderful person. . . ."

"Where did you meet him exactly?"

I'd told Kristine where I had met Desmond. I'd told her what he'd explained to me—he'd been offered a scholarship at Amherst, his father's college, but had deferred it for a year, at his request.

Kristine continued to question me about Desmond in a way I found offensive and condescending. I told her that she didn't know anything at all about Desmond, what he was like when we were alone together, how smart and funny he was, how thoughtful—"I think you're just jealous."

"Jealous! I am not."

"I think you are. You don't like to see me *happy*."

Kristine said, incensed: "Why would I be jealous of *him*? He's weird. His eyes are strange. I bet he's older than he says he is—at least twenty-three."

"Desmond is nineteen!"

"And you know this—how?"

"He told me. He took a year off between high school and college—he deferred going to Amherst this year."

"This year? Or some other year?"

"I think you're being ridiculous, and you're being mean."

"Also I think—I wouldn't be surprised—he's *gay.*"

This was a shock to me. Yet in a way not such a shock.

But I didn't want Kristine to know. I nearly shoved her away, furious.

"You know, Kristine—*I hate you.*"

Later, to my chagrin, I overheard Kristine talking with my mother in a serious tone about this "weird boy" who was "hanging out" with Lizbeth, who seemed "strange" to her.

Mom objected: "I think he's very nice. He's very well-mannered. You want your sister to have friends, don't you?"

"She has friends. She has great girlfriends."

"You want her to have a boyfriend, don't you? She's sixteen."

"Just that he'd be attracted to Lizbeth, who looks so young, and"—here Kristine hesitated, I knew she wanted to say that I wasn't pretty, wasn't attractive, only a weird boy would be interested in me—"isn't what you'd call 'experienced'—that seems suspicious to me."

"Kristine, you're being unfair. I've spoken with Desmond several times and he's always been extremely congenial. He's nothing like the high school boys around here—thank God. I'd like to have him to dinner sometime, with his parents. I think that would be very nice for Lizbeth."

"Not when I'm here, please! Count me out."

"I'd almost think, Krissie, that you're a little jealous of your younger sister. Among your friends there isn't anyone I've met who is anything like Desmond Parrish. . . ."

"He's *weird*. I think he's *gay*. It's OK to be weird and to be gay but not to hang around with my sister, please!"

"All right, Krissie. You've made your point."

"I'm just concerned about her, is all."

"Well, I think that Lizbeth can take care of herself. And I'm watching, too."

Kristine laughed derisively, as if she didn't think much of my mother's powers of observation.

"Dreams! The great mystery within."

On the redwood deck a few feet from us Rollo lay sprawled in the sun, asleep. His paws twitched and his gray muzzle moved as if, in his deep dog sleep, he was trying to talk.

"Animals dream. You can observe them. In his dream Rollo thinks he's running, maybe hunting. Retrievers are work dogs, hunting dogs. If not put to the use to which they've been bred they feel sad, incomplete. They feel as if part of their soul has been taken from them."

Desmond spoke with such certainty! I had never thought of Rollo in such a way.

He said, "Dreams are repositories of the day's memories. Or dreams are 'wish-fulfillment,' as Freud said. In which case there is a double meaning—a dream is the fulfillment of a wish, but the wish can be just a wish to remain asleep. So the dream lulls us into thinking we're already awake."

"Then what's the purpose of nightmares?"

"Must be, obviously, to punish."

To punish! I'd never thought of such a thing.

"Tell me about your dreams, Lizbeth. You haven't, yet."

In this, there was an air of slight reproach. Often now, Desmond spoke to me as if chiding me; as if there were such familiarity between us, he had no need to explain his mood.

I wondered if the meeting with Kristine was to blame. He knew that my sister wasn't *on his side*.

I had no idea what to say. Answering Desmond's questions was like answering questions in school: some teachers, though pretending otherwise, knew exactly what they wanted you to say; if you veered off in another direction, they disapproved.

"Well—I don't know. I can't make much sense of my dreams, mostly. For a while, when I was little, I thought they were real— I'd remember them as if they were real. I have a recurring dream of trying to run—stumbling, falling down. I'm trying desperately to get somewhere, and can't."

"And who is in your dreams?"

"Who? Oh—it could be anyone, or no one. Strangers."

We were sitting close together on a wicker sofa-swing on our redwood deck. Desmond's closeness was exciting to me in contemplation, when I was alone; when we were together, always there was something awkward about us. Desmond never slipped his arm around my shoulder or took my hand, except if he was helping me on a steep hiking trail; he hadn't yet brought his face close to mine though he "kissed" me good-bye—brushing his (cool, dry) lips against my cheek or my forehead as an adult might with a child.

I didn't want to think that what Kristine had said might be the explanation—Desmond wasn't attracted to me, in that way.

But then—why was he attracted to me at all?

Interrogating me now about my dreams as if this were a crucial subject. Why?

I told him that there was nothing special about my dreams that I could remember—"They're different every night. Sometimes just flashes and scraps of things, like a malfunctioning TV. Except if I have a nightmare . . ."

"What kind of nightmare?"

"Well—I don't know. It's always confusing and scary."

Desmond was staring at me so intently, I was beginning to feel uneasy.

"What sort of dreams have you been having recently? Has there been anything specific about them?"

How to answer this? I wasn't sure. It was almost impossible to remember a dream that evaporated so soon when you awoke.

"Well, I think that, a few times, I might have dreamt about —you. . . ."

I wasn't sure if this was true. But it seemed to be the answer Desmond was hoping for.

"Really! Me! What was I doing?"

"I—I don't remember. . . ."

The figure had been blurred. No face that I could see. But the hand had been uplifted, as if in greeting, or in warning. *Stay away. Don't come near.*

"When did you have this dream? Before you met me, or after?"

Desmond was gripping my arm at the wrist, as if not realizing how he squeezed me.

So it was not true that Desmond Parrish rarely touched me: at such times, he did.

Except this did not seem like *touch* but like—something else.

I wished that my mother would come outside, to bring us something to drink as she sometimes did. But maybe Mom wasn't in the kitchen, but in another part of the house.

Because Desmond dropped by without calling first, there was no way to know when he might show up. There was no way to arrange that someone else might be in the house, if I had wanted someone else to be in the house.

In our friendship, as I wanted to think of it, Desmond was always the one who made decisions: when we would meet, where we would go, what we would do. And if Desmond was busy elsewhere, if from time to time he had "things" to do in his own, private life, he just wouldn't show up—I didn't have a phone number to call.

He'd taken out the Polaroid camera, which I'd come to dislike.

"Did you have that dream before you met me? That would be wild!"

"I—I'm not sure. I think it was just the other night. . . ."

"Talk to me, Lizbeth. Tell me about your dreams. Like I'm your analyst, you're my *analysand*. That would be cool!"

As I tried seriously to recall a dream, as a submerged dream of the night before slowly materialized in my memory, like a cloudy Polaroid print taking a precise shape, Desmond took pictures of me, from unnervingly close by.

"There was a lake, a black lake . . . there were strange tangled-looking trees growing right out into the water, like a solid wall . . . we were in a canoe . . . I think it might have been you, paddling . . . but I'm not sure if it was me with you, exactly."

"Not you? What do you mean? Who was it, then?"

"I—I don't know."

"Silly! How can you have a dream in which you are not you? Who else would it be, paddling in a canoe at Lake Miskatonic, except me and you? You're my guest at our family lodge there— must be."

Desmond's voice was distracted as he regarded me through the camera viewfinder.

Click, click! He continued questioning me, and taking pictures, until I hid my face in my hands.

"Sorry! But I got some great shots, I think."

When I asked Desmond what his dreams were like he shrugged off the question.

"Don't know. My dreams have been taken from me, like my driver's license."

"How have your dreams been taken from you?"

"You'd have to ask the *Herr Doktors*."

I remembered that Desmond's father was a *Doktor*. But here was a reference to *Doktors*.

I wondered if Desmond had taken some sort of medication? I knew that a category of drugs called "psychoactive" could suppress dreams entirely. The mind became blank—an emptiness.

Desmond peered at the Polaroid images as they materialized. Whatever he saw, he decided not to share with me and put the pictures away in his backpack without a word.

I said it seemed sad, that he didn't dream any longer.

Desmond shrugged. "Sometimes it's better not to dream."

When Desmond left my house that day he drew his thumb gently across my forehead, at the temple. For a moment I thought he would kiss me there, my eyelids fluttered with expectation—but he didn't.

"You're still young enough, your dreams won't hurt you."

I thought it might be a mistake. But my eager mother could not be dissuaded.

She invited Desmond to have dinner with us and ask his parents to join us, and with a stiff little smile, as if the first pangs of migraine had struck behind his eyes, Desmond quickly declined: "Thanks, Mrs. Marsh! That's very generous of you. Except my parents are too busy right now. My father may even be traveling. And me—right now—it's just not a—not a good time."

My mother renewed the invitation another time, a few days later, but Desmond replied in the same way. I felt sorry for her, and unease about Desmond. Though when we were alone he had numerous questions to ask me about my family, as about myself, clearly he didn't want to meet them; nor did he want his parents to meet any of us, even his dear soul mate Lizbeth whom he claimed to adore.

It was near the end of October that Desmond brought his violin to our house and played for my mother and me.

This magical time! At least, it began that way.

In Desmond's fingers the beautiful little instrument looked small as a child's violin. "A little Mozart—for beginners."

Desmond bit his lower lip in concentration as he played, shutting his eyes. He moved the bow across the strings at first tentatively and then with more confidence. The beautiful notes wafted over my mother and me as we sat listening in admiration.

We were not strangers to amateur violin-playing—there were recitals in Strykersville in which both Kristine and I had partici-pated as piano students.

Possibly, some of Desmond's notes were scratchy. Possibly, the strings were not all fine-tuned. Desmond himself seemed piqued, and played passages a second time.

My mother said, "Desmond, that's wonderful! How long have you had lessons?"

"Eleven years, but not continuously. My last teacher said that I'm gifted—for an amateur."

"Are you taking lessons now?"

"No. Not here." Desmond's lips twitched in a faint smile as if this question was too naive to take seriously, but he would take it seriously. "I'm living in Strykersville now, not in Rochester. Or in Munich, or Trieste."

Meaning that there could be no violin instructor of merit in Strykersville.

My mother lingered for a while, listening to Desmond play. It was clear that she enjoyed Desmond's company more than the company of many of her friends. I felt a thrill of vindication, that my sister was mistaken about Desmond. I thought *Mom is on our side.*

When my mother left us, Desmond played an extraordinarily beautiful piece of music—"It's a transcription for violin. The 'Love-Death' theme from *Tristan und Isolde.*"

Though Desmond didn't play perfectly the emotional power of the music was unmistakable. I felt that I loved Desmond Parrish deeply— this would be the purest love of my life.

Desmond lowered the bow, smiling at me. His eyes behind the gold-rimmed lenses were earnest, eager.

"Now, you try, Lizbeth. I can guide you."

"Try? To play—what?"

"Just notes. Just—do what I instruct you."

"But—"

"You've had violin lessons. The technique will come back to you."

But I hadn't had violin lessons. I'd mentioned to Desmond that I had had piano lessons from the age of six to twelve, but I hadn't been very talented and no one had objected when I quit.

I protested, I couldn't begin to play a violin! The instrument was totally different from a piano.

"You've had music lessons, that's the main thing. The notes, the relationships between them—that's the principle of music. C'mon, Lizbeth—try!"

Desmond closed his hand around mine, gripping the bow, as he positioned the fragile instrument on my left shoulder.

Awkwardly Desmond caused the bow to move over the strings, gripping my fingers. The sounds were scratchy, shrill.

"Desmond, thanks. But—"

"I could teach you, Lizbeth. All that I know, I could impart to *you*."

"But—that isn't very realistic. . . ."

Sternly Desmond said: "Look. Playing a musical instrument requires patience, practice, and faith. It doesn't require great talent. So don't use that as an excuse—you aren't talented. *Of course you aren't talented*—that's beside the point." He spoke as if explaining something self-evident that only obstinacy prevented me from accepting.

"We could play together. Each with a violin. We could have a recital—people would applaud! But it requires patience."

The scraping noises of the violin, and Desmond's abrasive voice, caused Rollo to glance up at us from a few feet away, worriedly.

Desmond was wholly focused upon "instructing" me. This was a side of him I hadn't seen before—there was nothing tender about him now, only an air of determination. A smell of perspiration lifted from his underarms, there was an oily ooze on his forehead. He breathed quickly, audibly. Our nearness wasn't a comfort but intimidating. It was beginning to be upsetting that I couldn't seem to explain to this adamant young man that I really didn't want to take violin instructions from him, or from anyone.

When I tried to squirm away he squeezed my hand, hard—he was looming over me and his smile didn't seem so friendly now.

"You're not even trying for God's sake. Why do you just *give up*."

Hearing Desmond's voice, my mother appeared in the doorway.

Quickly then Desmond stammered an apology, took back the gleaming little violin from me, and left.

Mom and I stared after him, shaken.

"That voice I heard, Lizbeth—I'd swear, it wasn't Desmond."

Following this, something seemed to have altered between Desmond and me.

He didn't call. He began to appear in places I would not expect. He'd never made any effort to see me before school, only after school, once or twice a week at the most, but now I began to see him watching me from across the street when I entered school at about 8 A.M. If I waved shyly to him he didn't wave back but turned away as if he hadn't seen me.

"Is that your boyfriend over there? What's he doing there?"—my girlfriends would ask.

"We had a disagreement. He wants to make up. I think."

I tried to speak casually. I hoped the tremor in my voice wasn't detectable.

This was the sort of thing a girl would say, wasn't it?—a girl in my circumstances, with a *boyfriend*?

I realized that I had no idea what it meant, to have a *boyfriend*. Still more, *had a disagreement.*

And after school, Desmond began to appear closer to the building. He didn't seem to mind, as he'd initially minded, mingling with high school students as they moved past him in an erratic stream—Desmond a fixed point, like a rock. Waiting for me, then staring at me, not smiling, with a curt little wave of his hand as I approached—as if I might not have recognized him otherwise.

I'd gotten into the habit of hurrying from school on those days I didn't have a meeting or field hockey. It seemed urgent to get outside soon after the final bell. I didn't always want to be explaining Desmond to my friends. I didn't want always to be telling them that I had to hurry, my *boyfriend* wanted to see me alone.

Where Desmond hadn't shown any interest in watching me play field hockey now he might turn up at a game, or even at practice, not sitting in the bleachers with our (usually few) spectators; he preferred to remain aloof, standing at the edge of the playing field where he could stroll off unobserved at any time—except of course Desmond was observed, especially by me.

"When are you going to introduce Desmond to us, Lizbeth?"

"Is he kind of—the jealous type?"

"He looks like a preppy! He looks rich."

"He looks a little older like—a college guy, at least?"

It was thrilling to me that my friends and teammates knew that the tall lanky boy who kept his distance was my *boyfriend*—but not so thrilling that they must have been talking behind my back, speculating and even worrying about me.

There's some secret about him, Lizbeth won't tell.

Maybe Lizbeth doesn't know!

You think he's abusing her? You know—it could be mental, too.

Lizbeth is kind of changed, lately.

Does anybody know him? His family?

They're new to Strykersville. Lizbeth said.

She's crazy about him, that's obvious.

Or just kind of crazy.

You think he feels the same about her?

"I'm thinking maybe, I'll defer again—and wait for you. I have plenty of independent research I can do before going to college. And if you couldn't get into Amherst, or couldn't afford it—my dad could help out. What d'you think?"

For the first time, I lied to Desmond.

Then, for the second time, I lied to Desmond.

He hadn't been waiting for me at school but he'd come over to our house at about 6 P.M., rapped on the back door as he usually did, which led out onto the redwood deck, and when I came to the door I told him that I couldn't see him right then—"My mom needs me for something. I have to help her with something."

"Can't it wait? Or—can't I wait? How long will this 'something' require?"

I was so anxious, I hadn't even invited Desmond inside. Nor did I want to come outside onto the deck, which would make it more difficult for me to ease away from Desmond, and back into the house.

A thin cold rain was falling. A smell of wet rotting leaves.

Desmond had bicycled over. He was wearing a shiny yellow rain slicker, and a conical rain hat, which made him look both comical and threatening, like an alien life-form in a sci-fi horror movie.

"I said I can't, Desmond. This isn't a good time. . . . Daddy will be home soon, we're having dinner early tonight. There's some family crisis kind of thing going on, I can't tell you about— my elderly grandmother, in a nursing home . . ."

This was enough to discourage Desmond who had no more questions for me but backed off with a hurt smirk of a smile.

"Good night then, Lizbeth! Have a happy family crisis."

This sarcastic remark lingered in my memory like a taste of something rotten in my mouth.

I thought *He hates me now. I have lost him now.*

I thought *Thank God! He will find someone else.*

It happened then: Desmond Parrish drifted to the edge of my life.

He ceased coming to the house. He ceased waiting for me after school. His telephone calls that had been infrequent now ceased.

I felt his fury, at a distance.

He'd been insulted by my resistance to him. So subtle, another boy would scarcely have noticed. But of course Desmond Parrish wasn't *another boy*.

I regretted turning him away. I thought it might be the worst mistake of my life. When I received my amphibian paper back, in earth science, seeing a red A+ prominent on the first page, my first wish was to tell Desmond, who'd helped me with the paper.

So long ago, that seemed now! But it had been less than a month.

Desmond had read a draft of the paper for me and made just a few suggestions. He'd encouraged me to explore the theme of *amphibian* in a way not exclusively literal—" 'Ontology recapitulates philology.' If you don't know what that means, I can explain."

Now, all that was changed.

Now, I couldn't predict when I might see Desmond. He had removed himself from my life, decisively—but he was still *there,* observing.

In the corner of my eye I would see him. And in my uneasy dreams I would see him.

Walking with friends. Driving with my mother in her car.

One afternoon at the mall, with Kristine.

And another time, with Kristine, driving to a drugstore a half-mile from our house, in a shopping center, and there I saw, about thirty feet away, Desmond Parrish observing us: in his shiny yellow cyclist's helmet and a nylon parka and arms folded tight across his chest and when I stopped to stare the figure turned quickly away and vanished from my sight.

Seeing the look in my face Kristine said: "Are you all right, Lizzie? You look kind of sick."

I was so stricken by the sight of Desmond, I had to sit down for a few minutes.

Kristine asked, concerned, if I wanted to go home; but I said no, I did not want to go home. I did not!

"You've seemed kind of quiet lately."

I told her I was all right. But I had things to think about that couldn't be shared.

"About Des? Something about Des?"

Kristine knew that Desmond wasn't dropping by the house any longer. Nor did I speak of Desmond to her now, or to my mother.

"What's happened to him? Did you two break up?"

In Kristine's voice there was the equivalent of a smirk.

Break up. Your weird boyfriend.

My sister's condescending attitude made me want to slap her. For what did Kristine *know*.

It was so, Desmond frightened me now. Since he'd squeezed my hand so hard, gripping the violin bow, and since I'd sensed in him a willfulness that had no tenderness for me but only a wish to subjugate, I did not want to be in his presence: I began to tremble thinking of him.

Yet, perversely, I cherished the memory of my *boyfriend*. The memory of Desmond Parrish was more thrilling to me than Desmond himself had been in recent weeks.

"You didn't—make any mistakes with him, did you? Lizbeth?"

Kristine spoke hesitantly, embarrassed. We were not sisters who confided in each other about intimate things and we were not about to start now.

Gritting my teeth I told her no.

"He didn't coerce you into—or force you into—anything you didn't want to do—did he?"

Muttering no, I walked away from Kristine.

I wasn't sure if I wanted to shove her from me, or, ridiculously, push into her arms so she could comfort me as she'd done when I'd been a little girl.

"Maybe you thought you loved—love—him. But you didn't— you don't. . . ."

When we left the drugstore to cross the parking lot to my mother's station wagon, which Kristine was driving, in the corner of my eye I saw a tall lean figure wearing a yellow helmet in the rear exit of another store. It was the very figure I dreaded seeing, and dreaded not seeing.

I collapsed into the station wagon, my knees weak. I didn't turn to stare at the figure on the pavement, I didn't say a word to Kristine who reached out wordlessly to squeeze my hand.

Wistfully my mother said: "Lizbeth, what has happened to Desmond? Has he *disappeared*? He seemed so—devoted. . . ."

I knew that Mom was thinking *So devoted to both of us.*

YOU JUST CAN'T SHUT ME OUT OF YOUR LIFE LIZBETH YOU KNOW THAT WE ARE SOUL MATES FROM THAT OTHER LIFETIME

This message was left for me, in felt-tip black ink on a scroll of gilt paper, inside a plain white envelope, thrust into my high school locker.

I opened the gilt paper and read these words, stunned. I could not believe that Desmond had actually come into the school building, where he didn't belong; that he'd risked being detected, in order to observe me, at least once, who knows how many times, at my locker.

Then, to slip the envelope into my locker, he must have come after school when the corridor was deserted.

My hand trembled, holding the gilt scroll that looked like some kind of festive announcement.

Many times I would reread it. Many times in the secrecy of my room.

The message held a threat, I thought—or hinted at a threat.

I must tell my parents, I thought.

But they might try to contact Desmond's parents, or worse yet, the Strykersville police. . . . I did not want this.

Yet it wasn't clear how Desmond expected me to contact him. He had never given me his telephone number, or his address. It was as if we were gazing at each other across a deep ravine and had no way now of communicating except

SO NEAR   ANY TIME   ALWAYS

in broad, crude gestures like individuals who did not share
a language.

"Please! Just leave me alone."

He did call. I think it had to be him.

Late at night, and just a single ring, or two—if someone
picked up the phone, silence.

A taunting sort of silence into which words flutter and fall:
"Hello? Hello? Who is this. . . ."

He bicycled past our house, I think.

I think it was Desmond Parrish. I couldn't be sure.

A car pulled into our driveway, headlights blinding against
our windows. There was a rude blast of music. Then the car
pulled away again.

Then Rollo disappeared.

One night he failed to appear at the back door when we called
him, where usually Rollo was pawing the door to be allowed
back inside.

(Our acre-sized back lawn was fenced in so that Rollo could
spend as much time outdoors as he wanted. Usually, he just
slept on the deck.)

We scoured the neighborhood calling—"Rollo! Rollo!"

We rang doorbells. We photocopied flyers to staple to
trees, fences. We checked local animal shelters. Kristine came
home from Wells to help us search. We were distraught,
heartbroken.

I thought *Desmond would not do this. He would not be so cruel, he liked Rollo.*

I thought *Maybe he is keeping Rollo. Until I see him again.*

Now Desmond was *the stalker*—this was Kristine's term.

Suddenly it happened, he was always *there*. And others saw him, too.

Where previously, before Desmond, I'd often been alone, and comforted myself with self-pity that I was alone—now I could not ever be alone; I could not ever assume that I was alone. For I knew that Desmond Parrish was thinking about me obsessively, even when he wasn't actually watching me.

. . . Can't just shut me out. Soul mates from that other . . .

Hockey season was ending. This was a relief. For Desmond had begun showing up at practice, which was Thursdays after school. A lone lanky figure now behind the chain-link fence at the very rear of the playing field, arms uplifted and fingers caught in the links so that a quick glance made you think that whoever this was, he'd been crucified against the fence.

My teammates nudged me in the ribs, whispered to me.

"Hey, Lizbeth: is that your *boyfriend*?"

Or, "Looks like Lizbeth's *boyfriend* is stalking her."

Our coach called me into her office and spoke with me frankly. She said that my *boyfriend* was causing distraction and disruption—"You aren't playing very well, which is why I haven't sent you in much lately. And your distraction is bringing your teammates down."

Weakly I said, "He isn't my boyfriend. We broke up, I guess.
. . . I don't know why he's doing this."

"How close were you two? Were you—intimate?"

The question was like a slap in the face. To answer *no* seemed
pathetic. To answer *yes* would have been more pathetic.

I told Ms. DeLuca *no*. Not *intimate*.

"You're sure?" Ms. DeLuca regarded me suspiciously.

Yes, I was sure. But I spoke slowly, uncertainly. For just
to speak of Desmond with a stranger was a betrayal of our
true intimacy, which was like nothing else in my life until
that time.

"Lizbeth? Are you listening?"

"Y-Yes . . ."

"There has certainly been a change in you. Your eyes look
haunted. Did this boy abuse you in any way? Did he take advantage of you?"

I shook my head wordlessly. How I hated this woman who
wanted only to protect me!

"Well—do your parents know about him? They've met him—
have they?"

I murmured *yes* ambiguously. For after all, Mom knew Desmond well—or would have claimed that she did.

I'd never told my father. I was terrified of what my father
might say and do for I believed that, in his alarm at what was
happening, my father would blame *me*.

Finally, I left Ms. DeLuca's office. I wasn't sure if our awkward
conversation had ended, I just—left.

*   *   *

In a plain manila envelope addressed to LIZBETH at my street address he sent me photographs of myself taken with a zoom lens. These were not Polaroids but small matte photos: there I was, oblivious of the camera eye, climbing out of my mother's car, walking with friends on the sidewalk near school, playing field hockey. The most disturbing photo was of me inside our house, after dark in our lighted kitchen, talking with a blurred figure who must have been my mother.

On the back of this photo was written in block letters:

SO NEAR   ANY TIME   ALWAYS

I did not show anyone. I was terrified of how my family would react.

You did this! You invited this person into our lives.

How could you have been so careless? So blind, ignorant?

Terrible to see myself, a figure in another's imagination, of no more substance than a paper doll.

A figure at the mercy of the invisible/invincible photographer.

I stood at the window, staring out into the darkness of our backyard. At the farther end of our property were trees, a thick stand of trees, impenetrable in darkness as a wall.

I thought that Desmond must hide inside these trees, with his remarkable zoom lens.

He was a hunter. I was in his crosshairs.

I wanted to scream out the back door *I hate you! I wish you were dead! Give Rollo back to us! Leave us alone.*

Desperately I wanted to wake up and it would be six—seven?—weeks ago.

Before the library. Before I'd bicycled into town on a Saturday afternoon to take notes on the evolution of amphibians in a way to make of myself a *good dutiful student.*

And I would wake up to the relief that no one was following me—no one loved me.

Then, one day, when I was leaving school late, after a meeting, at dusk, there stood Desmond Parrish waiting for me.

"Hey, Lizbeth! Remember me?"

Desmond was smiling at me, in reproach. The muscles of his face were clenched, he was so angry with me.

"Haven't forgotten me, have you? Your friend Des."

I stammered that I didn't want to see him. I would have turned to run back into the school building but—I didn't want to insult him.

I didn't want to anger him further.

I could not move: my legs were weak, paralyzed.

"Know what I think, Lizbeth?—I think you've been avoiding me. We've had a misunderstanding. I want to honor that—I mean, your wish to avoid me. I am all for the 'rights of women'—a female is not *chattel.* But since your behavior is based upon a misunderstanding, the logical solution would be to clear it up. We need to talk. And I have a car, I can drive you home."

"You have a car? You have a license to drive?"

"I have a *car*. My father's car. I'd only need a license to drive if I intended to have an accident, or to violate a traffic law, which I don't intend."

"I—I can't, Desmond. I'm sorry."

Still, I couldn't move. My knees had lost all strength.

Desmond loomed above me smiling so hard that the lower part of his face appeared about to crack.

His jaws were unshaven. His smart gold-rimmed glasses were askew on his nose. His hair hadn't been cut in some time and had begun to straggle over his collar.

"Just come with me, Lizbeth. We'll take a little drive—to the lake—the lake right here—remember, the canoes? You wanted to go out in a canoe, but then you were afraid? You were silly— you were afraid. But there's nothing to be afraid of. We can go there—we can try again. Then I'll drive you home. I promise. We need to talk."

Desperately I said that it was too late in the season, the boat rental wouldn't be open in November. And it was too late in the day, it was dark . . .

Foolishly I was protesting. As if renting a canoe was the point when clearly Desmond wanted to take me with him—wherever he had in mind.

There was in fact a vehicle parked nearby; headlights on, motor running, and driver's door flung open as if the driver had just leapt out.

Desmond dared to come forward and take hold of my arm.

Desmond dared to taunt me, in a mock-tender voice.

"I've heard your dog is lost. That's a tragedy—you love that dog. All of you love that dog. Might be, I could help you look for him. Was it—Rollo? Named for Rollo May? Cool!"

I had no idea what Desmond was saying, only just that he had Rollo. He knew where Rollo was.

Yet, he was pulling me toward the car. Instinctively I resisted.

"No. I don't want to go with you!"

"Don't be ridiculous, Lizbeth. Of course you want to come with me—if I can lead you to Rollo. And we can go to the lake —Little Huron Lake. In less than an hour this will all be cleared up and we'll be friends again."

I tried to disengage my arm from Desmond. His fingers gripped me tight.

My voice was pleading: "What do you want with me? Why are you doing this?"

"'What do I want with you'—what do you want with *me*! We are destined for each other as I knew at first sight, Lizbeth—and so did you."

Panicked I thought *This is not real. This is not happening.*

I thought *The boyfriend!*

Even with the lure of finding Rollo, I knew that I must not get into that car with Desmond Parrish.

Desmond cursed me, as I'd never heard him curse before. I was reminded of my mother remarking that the voice she'd heard on our deck hadn't been Desmond's voice but the voice of another.

Desmond was grappling with me, pinning my arms against my sides, half-carrying me to his car. I could feel his hot breath in my face. I could smell his body—the hot sweaty urgency of a male body. I was too frightened to scream. I could not draw breath to scream.

Then someone saw us, shouted at us, and Desmond quickly released me, ran to his car and drove away.

"Who was that? What was he trying to do to you?"—one of the vocational arts teachers was asking me.

I told him it was all right: I told him it was a misunderstanding. "Should I call 911?"

"No! No, please. It's just my boyfriend—but things will be all right now."

I was upstairs in my room when my mother called up to me, sounding hysterical.

On the local ten o'clock news it was announced that a Strykersville resident, Desmond Parrish, had died in a single-vehicle accident on the thruway. His car, driven at an estimated eighty miles an hour, had crashed into a concrete overpass six miles south of Strykersville.

We stared at film footage of the wreck, partly obscured by the flashing lights of medical vehicles and flares set in the left lane of the interstate highway. A young woman newscaster was saying solemnly that death was believed to have been "instantaneous."

We stared at a photograph of Desmond Parrish looking very young, with schoolboy eyeglasses and a knife-sharp part in his hair.

"That can't be Desmond! I don't believe this. . . ."

My mother was more upset than I was. My mother was gripping my hands to console me but my hands were limp and cold and unresponsive.

I was too shocked to comprehend most of the news. The "breaking news" bulletin passed so swiftly, within a few seconds it had ended and was supplanted by an advertisement.

My mother embraced me, weeping. I held myself stiff and unyielding.

I was waiting for the phone to ring: for Desmond to call, a final taunting time.

That night I dreamt of Little Huron Lake rippling in darkness.

In the morning we read in the Strykersville paper a more detailed account of how Desmond Parrish had died.

The front-page article contained another photograph of Desmond taken years before, looking very young. Again, Desmond wasn't smiling.

The photograph ran above the terrible headline:

STRYKERSVILLE RESIDENT, 22, DIES IN THRUWAY CRASH

Witnesses of the "accident" reported to state troopers that the speeding vehicle seemed to have been accelerating when the driver "lost control," slammed through a guardrail, and struck the concrete abutment head-on. No signs of skidding had been detected on the pavement.

The wrecked automobile, a 1977 Mercedes-Benz, was registered in the name of Gordon Parrish, Desmond's father.

Desmond Parrish had been driving without a license. At the time of the crash his parents had not known where he was: he'd been "missing from the house" since the afternoon.

Again it was stated: "Death is believed to have been instantaneous."

New York State police would be investigating the crash, which occurred outside the jurisdiction of the Strykersville police department.

Soon after, a woman who identified herself as a detective with the New York State Police came to our house to speak with me and my parents.

The detective informed us that a "cache" of photographs and "journal entries" concerning me had been recovered from the wrecked car.

Police were investigating the possibility that Desmond Parrish had committed suicide. The detective asked me if I had been "intimate" with Desmond Parrish; how long had I known Desmond Parrish, and in what capacity; when had I seen him last; what had been his state of mind when I'd seen him.

Calmly I replied. Tried to reply. I was aware of my parents listening to me, astonished.

Astonished and disapproving. For I had betrayed them, in not sharing with them all that had passed between my *boyfriend* and me.

Never after this would they trust me wholly. Never after this would my father regard me, as he'd liked to regard me in the past, as his *little girl.*

For instance, my parents hadn't known that Desmond had been "stalking" me—that he'd left a threatening message in my locker at school. They hadn't known that I'd seen Desmond so recently, on the very day of his death.

They hadn't known that he'd wanted me to come with him in that car, to drive to Little Huron Lake.

I would give a statement to police: Desmond had confronted me behind our school building at about 5:20 P.M. By 9:20 P.M. he had died.

The vocational arts teacher who'd come up behind us, who'd surprised and frightened Desmond away, would give a statement to police officers, also.

There'd been an "altercation" between Desmond Parrish and the sixteen-year-old high school sophomore Lizbeth Marsh. But Ms. Marsh had not wanted the teacher to call 911, and Mr. Parrish had driven away in his father's Mercedes.

It was believed that prior to the crash he'd "ingested" a quantity of alcohol. He had been driving without a license.

The detective told us that the Parrishes refused to believe that their son may have caused his own death deliberately. At the present time, they were not speaking with police officers and were "not accessible" to the media.

It would be their theory, issued through a lawyer, that their son had had an accident: he'd been drinking, he had not ever drunk to excess before and wasn't accustomed to alcohol, he'd had "personal issues" that had led to his drinking and so had "lost control" of the car and died.

He had not been suicidal, they insisted.

He had so much to live for, since moving to Strykersville.

He was seeing a therapist, and he'd been "making progress." He had not ever spoken of suicide, they insisted.

He'd had a "brilliant future," in fact. A scholarship to Amherst College, to study classics.

"You know, I hope, about Desmond's background? His criminal record?"

Criminal record?

We were utterly stunned by the detective's remark.

She told us that Desmond had been incarcerated from the age of fourteen to the age of twenty-one in the Brigham Men's Facility for Youthful Offenders in Brigham, Massachusetts. He'd pleaded guilty to voluntary manslaughter in the death of his eleven-year-old sister in August 1970.

All that was known of the incident was that Desmond, fourteen at the time, had been canoeing with his sister Amanda on Lake Miskatonic, where the Parrishes had a summer lodge, when in a "sudden fit of rage" he'd attacked her with the paddle, beat her about the head and chest until she died, and tried without success to push her body into the lake without capsizing the canoe. No one had witnessed the murder but the boy had been found in the drifting canoe, with his sister's bloodied corpse and the bloodied and splintered paddle, in a catatonic state.

Desmond had never explained clearly why he'd killed his sister except she'd made him "mad"; he'd had a quick temper since early childhood and had been variously diagnosed as suffering from attention deficit disorder, childhood schizophrenia, even autism. He'd been "unusually close" to his sister and had played violin duets with her. His parents had hired a lawyer to defend him against charges of second-degree homicide. After months of negotiations he'd been allowed to plead guilty to a lesser charge of manslaughter and was sentenced to seven years in the youth facility, which also contained a unit for psychiatric subjects, from which offenders were automatically released at the age of twenty-one.

This was a ridiculous statute, the prosecution claimed—anyone who'd committed such a "vicious" murder should not be released into society after just seven years. But Desmond was too young at fourteen to be tried as an adult. He'd been diagnosed as undeniably ill—mentally ill—but in the facility he'd responded well to therapy and was declared, by the time of his twenty-first birthday, to pose no clear and present danger to himself or others.

The family had relocated to Strykersville, within commuting distance of Rochester. It was hoped that the family, as well as Desmond, would make a "new start" here.

The Parrishes had never lived in Europe. Mr. Parrish had never helped to establish branches of Nord Pharmaceuticals in Europe. His position with the corporation was director of research in Rochester, exclusively.

The detective showed me a photograph of Amanda Parrish. Did she resemble me, did I resemble her, I don't think so. I heard my mother draw in her breath sharply seeing the photograph but I did not think that we looked so much alike. This girl was very young, really just a child, with a plain sweet hopeful face, unless you could call it a doomed face, those eyes, haunted eyes you could call them, that set of the mouth, a shy smile for the camera that might even have been held by her murderous older brother.

I thought of Desmond's warning about smiling for the camera. How foolish, how sad you will appear, when the smiling photograph appears posthumously.

The child/sister murder had been a celebrated case in the Miskatonic Valley, since the Parrish family was well known there, had owned property in the region since Revolutionary times.

"A tragic case. But these cases are not so rare as you might think."

It was a curious remark for the New York State police detective to make to us at such a time.

My father became livid with rage. My mother was upset, incredulous. They wanted to immediately confront the Parrishes, to demand an explanation.

"Those terrible people! How could they have been so selfish! They allowed their sick, disturbed son to behave as if he were normal. They must have known that he was seeing our daughter! They must have known that the medications he was taking weren't enough. They couldn't have been monitoring their son. . . ."

It was chilling to think that the Parrishes had been willing to risk my life, or to sacrifice my life, the life of a girl they didn't

know, had never met but must have known about—their son's
girlfriend.

They would never consent to speak with us. They would consent only to communicate through lawyers.

At that time I could not answer any more of the detective's
questions. I could not bear my parents' emotions. I ran away
from the adults, upstairs to my room.

I hid in my bed. I burrowed in my bed.

So often I'd dreamt of Desmond Parrish in this bed, it was
almost as if he were here with me: waiting for me.

I thought *He wanted to take me with him. He loved me—he
would not have hurt me.*

In Strykersville today there are too many memories. I never
remain more than a night or two, visiting my parents.

I try to avoid driving in the vicinity of Fort Huron Park. Never
would I revisit Little Huron Lake.

The remainder of my high school years is a blur to me. In the
summer I went to live with my grandmother in White Plains,
and there I took summer courses at Vassar; my senior year, I
transferred to a private school in White Plains, since my parents
thought it might be best to remove me from Strykersville, where
I had "emotional issues."

My old life was uprooted. My old "young" life.

I thought of wasps in our back lawn, their nests burrowed into
the ground into which my father would pour liquid insecticide.
In terror wasps would fly out of the burrow, fly to save their lives,

dazed, desperate. I wonder if the wasps could reestablish a nest elsewhere. I wondered if the poison had seeped into their frantic little insect-bodies, if mere escape were enough to save them.

I missed my friends, my family. I missed the life we'd had there, our sleepy old dog stretched out on the redwood deck at our feet. But I could not have remained in Strykersville where there were too many memories.

The other day I saw him. Across a busy street I saw his hand uplifted and in his face an expression of reproach and hurt and without thinking I began to cross the street to him, and at once horns sounded angrily—I'd stepped off the curb into traffic, and had almost been killed.

So near   any time   always

Rollo's body was never recovered.

THE EXECUTION

She'd said *You will have to speak with your father. I can't intercede for you any longer.*

He left the Delt-Sig house at 1:20 A.M., which was later than he'd planned. Half the house lighted like some weird kind of lopsided birthday cake, which didn't mean that all the guys were awake or fully conscious but only that scattered lights were left on including lights in the front foyer, the kitchen, and the steps to the grungy basement.

All this was planned. He'd given her the one final chance.

Shutting the cell phone on her shrill rising voice *Bart? Bart? Don't you dare cut me—*

Placed a call to DeMarco's. Pre-ordering eight large pizzas for 10 P.M. the following evening, deliver to the Delt-Sig house at 3992 Stadium Way. Party time!

He'd be paying with a Visa Platinum card, which, by that time, 10 P.M. of the next day, he would have in his possession, he was pretty sure. Or, by then—(he was vague about this)—his own Visa account might be reactivated.

Eight large pizzas for an estimated fifty to seventy-five guests.

The Explorer was parked in the alley behind the frat house. A prominent sign DO NOT PARK HERE VIOLATORS WILL BE TOWED had been bent and twisted and rendered harmless.

Can't intercede for you any longer didn't I tell you this would happen.

Your credit has been cut off. Your father warned you.

Gloves! Almost forgot the damn gloves.

Not a good pair of his own just a—this kind of cheap black *faux*-leather gloves he'd found jammed in somebody's parka hanging from a peg somewhere on campus.

So they would marvel *No fingerprints! Not a single fingerprint has been recovered at the crime scene.*

Black gloves tight-fitting at the knuckles. Black hoodie, black T-shirt, black jeans, black Nikes. Dark-tinted glasses, his eyes were freaky-dilated from the Ritalin and light from oncoming headlights could give him a headache.

High on Ritalin he'd planned each minute. Nothing impulsive about the *I B S*—code-name for the Execution.

Every minute he'd planned. Fuck, every *second*.

Every *nanosecond*.

And no witnesses!

That was crucial to the execution: no *witnesses*.

Planned the drive. Every exit he'd pass on the drive east.

Exits from Syracuse he knew by heart. Set the Explorer to cruise control seventy miles per hour but sometimes he drove faster, passing in the left lane. Christ, he loves this SUV! Like his actual *soul* is outside him, and he can *climb inside.*

Held the road steady as a tank. Bulled past eighteen-rigs like they were compacts.

Three hours and twenty minutes east on the thruway to the Rensselaer exit then into the Village of East Rensselaer to the stone Tudor house at 29 Juniper Drive almost invisible from the narrow road beneath the massed foliage of trees impenetrable as a wall.

Just the place—showy fake-Tudor, "cul-de-sac" and lots of evergreens—home invaders would target.

He was excited, which was a good feeling. Like at the start of a new game—like, *Brink* or *Day of Doom*—before you know what the terrain is, how fast it's going to rush at you, and how you will fuck up.

I B S is Bart's (secret) game. It will be flawless for, unlike a video game, put together by kinky-twisted genius-minds, *I B S* is Bart Hansen's creation.

He was feeling excited but also a little sulky, sullen. Thinking *See I gave you every chance. Both of you.*

He had! All his young life he'd been jerked on their short leash like a dog—fucking neck is raw and bleeding from the tight collar.

On Juniper Drive he cut the headlights approaching the house. Knowing how when a vehicle turned into the driveway at night headlights flashed up to the second-floor windows of their bedroom.

It was 4:28 A.M. Later than he'd originally planned but he was flexible. On the drive back he'd make up some of the lost time, he could relax then with the Execution behind him.

Parked in the circular driveway the gleaming black Explorer facing Juniper Drive for a quick escape.

He had his house key. Sure. No problem about letting himself in—quietly—but he knew the Vector Security system was *on*, this was how paranoid his father was.

Overhead a shredded-looking sky like old Kleenex. And a faint moon rising.

Made him shiver! The look of the moon, a stirring of hairs at the nape of his neck. He'd seen DVDs of *Werewolf of London*, *I Was a Teenaged Werewolf*, *The Wolfman* as a little kid, so many times that the discs had worn out.

He would enter the house through the garage. Darkly handsome in his black *Terminator* clothing.

It was hard not to see himself on video—YouTube. Stealthy-quick and silent as a panther and unerring.

There were three sliding overhead garage doors of which one had been left carelessly open. Bart's father had complained for years that his mother didn't lower the garage door after she'd parked her car inside—often, his mother didn't trouble to drive her car inside the garage. She'd scraped the sides of her car too frequently—she didn't think it was *so crucial*.

Burglary in the Village of East Rensselaer was rare. House break-ins, rare.

Still, Bart's father wanted the garage doors shut. And Bart's father wanted the Vector Security *on*.

On the rear garage wall he sees it: the ax.

Jesus! Sighting it with the beam of his flashlight, and he feels a deep shudder in his gut.

Hanging from a spike on the wall. Wood handle, with a sharp-looking edge. Lean and mean.

Has to weigh fifteen, twenty pounds.

This will be Bart's first time wielding the ax. He'd meant to rehearse—a practice session—never got around to it.

Dad had used the ax chopping firewood for the family-room fireplace.

Take it, Bart! Try it. Work up a little sweat.

In gloved hands he disengaged the ax from the wall. Heavy!

In the funnel-light of the flashlight he's surprised—a little shocked—to see spilling out of a corner of the garage so many of *his things*. Not just his bicycles—a half-dozen—the most recent an Italian racer, fifteen speeds, three thousand dollars but the tires were flat, he hadn't ridden it in a year or more—also old video games, play stations, electronic toys from when he'd been a little kid, even a Junior Jeep he'd been given for Christmas when he was five or six—he'd been crazy for that Junior Jeep until it broke down and never got repaired.

All this crap maybe they'd loved him when you calculated the sum total but now it's too late—*Fuck it.*

In gloved hands carrying the ax into the house.

Trying not to feel—this is weird—this is not-right—that the ax, in his hands, weighing down his arms, has a *life of its own,* he'd disturbed when he'd taken it down from the wall.

First step is to "disarm" the burglar alarm. He'd practiced this. Entering the house even with your key when the alarm is set you have ten seconds—T E N S E C O N D S— to get to the little box on the kitchen wall and punch in the code.

Part of the code was Dad's birth date—*1957.*

A few embarrassing times it had happened, alarms in the house had gone off by accident.

The burglar alarm, the smoke detector. One was a high-pitched deafening siren, the other a deafening *beep-beep-beep.*

Now it was crucial to move swiftly but not to hurry. Hurrying you only fuck things up.

He'd taken three Rits. He'd had just a few beers at the Delt-Sig house. The pizza, with slimy-salty anchovies, was feeling heavy in his gut like it hadn't been chewed—"masticated"—but was a single doughy lump.

The Delt-Sigs who were Bart's friends gave him a place to crash, anytime. *It's shitty you're on probation this semester but there's always a place here for you.*

Not the fraternity officers. They weren't Bart's particular friends. But the other guys, who'd pledged with him. And Bart's Big Brother Shaugh.

Why he wanted to repay them. Hell, he'd invite all of them.

The next night, there'd be something to celebrate and Bart Hansen would be hosting the party. Pizza, beer, any kind of party snack—tacos, spicy dip—raw oysters on the half-shell—those big jumbo shrimps you dip in red sauce—thinking of it made his mouth water and his heart swell with pride the guys would be impressed, the girls would be impressed as hell—he'd get on the phone tomorrow afternoon and make more calls.

He'd have the Visa Platinum then. Or—whatever. Maybe cash he'd hand to the delivery kid, see the look on his face.

Delt-Sigs were known for their wild keg parties. On the Hill the frats with party reputations were Kappa Eps, TriThetas, Pi-Betas, and Delt-Sigs.

From a block away you could hear the Delt-Sig house blaring music weekend nights—*Metallica, Black Sabbath.*

At the Delt-Sig house was a prevailing smell of stale beer, stale piss, stale pizza crusts. Saturating the rugs, draperies, wallpaper.

All he's had to eat in twenty-four hours is pizza the guys ordered—not from DeMarco's, which is high quality—pepperoni sausage swimming in grease, clotted cheese, anchovies—who the hell always orders anchovies?—Christ! He hates the things, spits them out if he can.

He's putting on weight, that's a downer. Pale-doughy fat around his waist like his old man, he's only *twenty.*

Academic suspension for the spring semester since he'd flunked three courses last semester. The previous suspension, Bart's sophomore year, was expunged from his university record.

Expunged. He did owe that to Dad—Dad's lawyer meeting with the university lawyer.

One of the courses he'd supposedly flunked was Computer 101. This was a joke! The labs were taught by Pakistanis or Chinese speaking some gibberish you could not comprehend. And in Bart's case, this Ahal, or Ahab, or Aheel had been biased against the white frat guys from the first meeting, Bart had protested to his adviser and to the chair of the computer department and to the dean of students and finally to his parents—hell of a lot of good the effort did him.

Well—his mother had been sympathetic. But hell of a lot of good that did *him*.

Gritting his teeth he's so—*intense*. Excited, or angry. Might be the Ritalin, or adrenaline. Fast-running sensation like something red-hot molten in the veins—wild!

Like ascending in a balloon—fast.

His ninth birthday his parents had arranged a balloon ride for Bart and his little friends.

So excited, but also scared. Too scared to climb into the basket with the other boys.

So panicked he'd wet his God damn jeans. Crying and ashamed and Mommy had to comfort him while the other boys went up in the balloon squealing and shouting—*so ashamed*.

Afterward no one spoke of it. But in his heart like a tiny thorn a hatred of Dad who'd made such a big deal of the fucking balloon ride.

They hadn't wanted him to have the Explorer either. Try to explain it was *pre-owned not new!*

He'd gotten the best deal. Sexy-black, four-wheel drive, curve control. Seven-passenger capacity.

Delt-Sig hosted winter-blast parties at Elkhorn Lake. For Adirondack roads in winter you need four-wheel drive and you need SUV-size seating.

He'd planned: Wednesday. Middle of the week, and slow.

Thursday was pretty much party night on the Hill—fraternity row. You couldn't plan anything serious for that night.

The party Bart would give, with not just pizzas and beer but fancier expensive party food, was the first step of reparation. For he was in debt to the Delt-Sig house, big time.

He'd tried to explain to his parents.

Mom had been sympathetic, more than Dad. But in the end, she'd let him down like the old man.

All the guys said the same thing—your mom will side with you when your old man will not but in the end, including even if they're divorced, your mom will side with the old man because that's where the cash is.

So meticulously he'd planned. Like for instance the pocket flashlight, the surveillance-disarming. But he'd made a major fuck-up not realizing at the time, but later, oh Christ he could kick himself in the ass he screwed up *taking the thruway not back roads.*

Just didn't think of it! Did not think of it.

Fucking thruway where he used his E-ZPass. Fixed to the windshield. So automatic he never gave it a thought. His E-ZPass account was billed to his parents' account, he never saw the bills and never gave it a thought.

Nor the surveillance cameras on the thruway—never gave it a thought.

Just didn't think. That was what they'd been bitching about him—the past ten years—*Just didn't think did you!*

Well—Bart has thought now. Bart has thought very carefully. Bart has thought with the desperate cunning of a rat in a trap knowing he must free himself from the trap, or die.

The ax just came to him. Planning *I B S* when he'd been a young kid he'd fantasized AK-47s, grenades, or machetes—firebombing the house—now he's twenty years old, he's more realistic.

In the Delt-Sig house a couple of weeks ago he'd woken from a drunk sleep with a taste of vomit in his mouth like yellow acid and the first thing was—(must've been he'd dreamt this)—the ax hanging from a spike in the garage came floating to him, the idea of the ax, his hands reached out to grip the ax firmly as—(must've memorized this years ago)—he'd envisioned wresting the ax from his father's hands when Dad was chopping firewood out back of the house *thud! thud! thud!* In the sharp wintry air his breath steaming. Dad had said his father, that is, Bart's grandfather, used to chop firewood like this at the farm in Elmira and he, that is, Bart's father, had always helped him, and how fast you work up a sweat, it's great exercise.

Want to spell me, try chopping a while you'll get to like it, Bart.

You might need gloves, though. Any gloves handy?

Bart had said OK, Dad. Some other time.

Laugh-out-loud, such bullshit.

It was always like that: Bart's father trying to coerce him into doing something he used to do when he was a kid, so Bart is supposed to fall in line and do it, too; and if he doesn't, or won't, Dad gets pissed and looks at him *that way.*

Home invasion like in Connecticut: two guys break into a suburban house, terrorize the mother and two teenaged daughters, rape and beat them, and tie them to a bed and sprinkle gasoline and light it—house goes up in a blaze! They didn't get the father, just the mother and girls. Stupid fuckers, ex-cons, *got caught.*

A few years ago there'd been thefts at 29 Juniper Drive also at neighbors' homes—25 Juniper Drive, 31 Juniper Drive—computers, electronic equipment, video games, silver candlestick holders—but the perpetrator had been identified, the stolen items returned or anyway most of them, financial reimbursement made, no charges filed with police.

Negotiating with the neighbors not to press charges. Bart's mother had been so ashamed—she'd said, how many times. Sure, and Bart was sorry, too—he'd needed the money bad, junior year in high school. Bart's father had never forgiven him, just one more fucking thing he'd held against him like the check for the Explorer—already, a thousand times he'd brought up that—*throwing it in his face every chance he could though Bart had said he was sorry how many fucking times, did they want him to immolate himself?*

He'd had a drug problem, high school. He'd gone to rehab. It was OK. The family judge, a female, was understanding. And Mom was understanding—*as long as this never happens again, Bart.*

He'd swore, it would never happen again.

That crummy crap he'd taken from his parents and the neighbors hadn't been worth the effort and the risk for less than five hundred bucks and the dope he'd blown it on hadn't made any special impression on the people he'd hoped to impress—for sure, that shit would never happen again.

And yes, *he was sorry.*

It's like the ax is leading him. Upstairs.

Gripped in his (gloved) hands. Metallica screaming in his ears *Die, die, die my darling.*

Past the doorway of his (darkened) room. And the door is partway open like someone is inside—who?

Soon, he won't remember that punk kid. Scared of his shadow practically, fucking *ashamed.*

In a weird movie—like *Inception*—could be *Bart Hansen is in his room, asleep in his bed and all outside is his dream unfolding.*

Like *Matrix. Bourne Conspiracy.* Some kind of mind-fuck. You can argue you are not responsible.

You can argue *you are not you.*

It's an idea: his generation. Nobody is who they're supposed to be—who older people want them to be. A click, a twist of the dial—*you're gone.*

At their (closed) door. As a little kid he'd stood outside this door plenty of times.

Just reaches out, grips the doorknob and—turns it. . . .

Opens the door and—

Like some kind of explosion like a—suicide bomb—the door is pushed, there's his father confronting him, Dad in pajama bottoms and no top so his hairy-fatty chest is exposed and his face livid with shock, rage—*Bart! What the hell are*—

Like Dad did not see the ax for Christ's sake.

Or seeing the ax discounted it thinking *The kid will screw up, the kid can't do a fucking thing right.*

This loud voice like a bullhorn in Bart's ears, a shock after so much quiet, almost he'd come to think this was in fact his dream, and nobody in it except him. Then this loud-mouth furious man yelling at him, demanding of him what the hell he thinks he is doing creeping into the house is he intending to steal from them again, God damn says Dad he's going to call the police—

And there is the mother in bed a few yards away, sitting up confused—and seeing them struggling in the doorway, Bart in black hoodie and black jeans, his face exposed when his father had switched on the overhead light—the ax between them, lifting and plunging with its own terrible energy—she opens her mouth to scream—

So it happens for all his meticulous planning Bart has no choice bringing the sharp side of the ax down against Dad's skull, Dad's furious face, as the older man sinks at once like a felled tree, all resistance gone, in an instant gone, a look of perplexity and wonder in his bleeding face, both his hands clutching at his son who flails blindly at him with the ax—*Get away, get away from me*—sharp edge of the ax, blunt edge of the ax, sharp edge, blunt edge, as Bart swings blindly until on the floor the bleeding figure is tangled in Bart's feet—he's panicked kicking free Oh Christ!—what has happened he didn't intend *this.* A deafening roar in his ears but he knows he has to get to the woman in the bed, that is the next step, he must execute the second step, bring down the woman struggling to escape from the bed and into the bathroom where she will lock the door and he will have to shred the door with the ax—rushing at her, jumping up onto the bed as he has not done since he's been a young child daringly climbing up onto his parents' bed and bouncing on it now swinging the ax at the woman in a wide careening arc—missing her, almost losing his balance—panting—not the sharp side of the weapon but the blunt side, Bart can't bring himself to strike his mother with the terrible sharp edge of the ax for she is begging him *No Bart no honey please no* for he'd gotten along mostly OK with Mom, mainly he was pissed she hadn't defended him enough against his father, God damn she'd let him down too many times culminating in the loan fiasco for the SUV, she'd helped him with Delt-Sig dues and fees, some other debts he'd owed, from her own checking account and the father hadn't known, or hadn't been supposed to know, but somehow that got screwed up, the father had seen the bank statement and called Bart on his cell leaving messages increasingly threatening, speaking of the police, *taking the matter to the police* so Bart has no choice but to act as he is acting—no choice as a trapped rat has no choice—but the fact is: he'd stunned them first with the ax, blunt side against their skulls to stun them like you would stun a cow before slaughter so it's a merciful death, they *never felt a thing*.

Next he knew the heavy ax had slithered from his hands. Had the bloodied ax head flown off?

Just the wood handle in his hands, he uses to push at the— the thing on the floor—the man with the split skull, gushing blood—and the thing on the bed—he will cover with bedclothes. Dragging sheets and blankets from the bed, dragging a blanket over the thing on the floor scarcely recognizable as his father, face split in bloody halves like a mangled pumpkin, and the lacerated neck spouting blood—dragging a blanket to hide it. And the other—the woman—half-naked, fleshy and smelling of bowels—an alarming stench— part of her upper skull missing— right eye mashed out of its socket —still she's begging *No honey no p-please noooo*—blood like a great black rose enveloping her where she has fallen slantwise on the bed, already the bedclothes are dark-stained, he has to swallow hard not to puke up his guts dragging a quilt over the woman, to hide her; the quivering body, the shuddering female body, he places pillows, satin pillows, and from her bathroom, which is adjoining the bedroom, he grabs as many towels as he can, heaped atop her in layers.

Die die die my darling. Don't utter a single word.

He's panting, as if he's been sprinting a mile race. His gut aches.

It would begin now: the ceaseless sensation of movement, motion, as of hot gaseous liquids, in his lower gut.

Ceaseless seething, fizzing. At first it was, like, his stomach was *growling*—which was a kind of joke—a kid joke, like farting—then, as hours passed, days, eventually weeks, gas pains like knife stabs coming one-two-three in quick sensation so he felt the blood drain from his face, so he almost fainted. *What has happened to me, something is eating me from inside*—it was like something had burrowed into him, a snake, a giant slug, rapacious and insatiable eating him from inside.

The weird thing was, the ax had taken on its own willful life almost immediately swinging out of his control, careening in wider and more extravagant arcs than Bart would have been capable of until the ax head flew off the handle and he'd dropped the handle in horror on the floor amid the tangled bedclothes, bloodied bodies and one of them—it had to be Louisa—moaning from beneath the quilt, pillows and towels he'd heaped on her quivering body in the hope that she would suffocate and die faster *and pass out of her misery.*

For another weird thing was, Bart would never share with anyone, once he'd used the ax on both his parents and the ax head had flown off the handle, he could not strike them again not even with the handle. He *could not.*

No fingerprints. The assailant had worn gloves.

No *physical evidence*. The assailant had acted swiftly and shrewdly and had left no sign of himself behind.

Obviously a break-in, attempted burglary that had gone wrong.

Whoever the killer was, he'd decided not to take anything.

(For Bart reasoned: whatever he took from his parents' house if he tried to sell it, or barter it, or pawn it—he'd be caught. That was a major blunder he wasn't going to make.)

It was a part of the execution plan—*I B S*—to change his clothes *after*.

Shower, quick. In his father's bathroom not his own for he knows that would be a mistake—shower floor damp, towels damp, sink recently used. All he takes from his own room—from his bureau, his closet—is a change of clothes—dark clothes to replace the filthy clothes he's going to wrap in a bundle and drop in a Dumpster at a lonely exit on the thruway on the drive home. (He hasn't planned the exit. That, he will leave to chance. But it will turn out to be exit 19 at Skaggsville almost exactly equidistant from East Rensselaer and Syracuse, a rest-stop Dumpster, which will be a tactical error since such Dumpsters are emptied less frequently than, for instance, a Dumpster behind a McDonald's or Wendy's, and Rensselaer police will discover the bundle within forty-eight hours.) There's video games he'd have liked to take back to Syracuse with him from a shelf in his room, *Dead Space 2, Portal 2,* and *Brink,* which is awesome but no better not—he's superstitious. Doesn't want to do anything in this room beyond the bare necessity of getting clean clothes, which is why there will be *no physical evidence*.

Why the blogs will be saying of Bart Hansen *he's one smart kid. Darkly handsome. Charismatic, generous—party-loving.*

Every teacher Bart had ever had, every relative of his, neighbor —friend of the Hansen family—assured the worried parents your son is a smart kid if he'd only just *apply himself.*

K through twelfth grade at Rensselaer Day School, more or less that was the consensus—*Bart Hansen is a smart kid if only he'd apply himself.*

He'd been a promising athlete. Middle school, upper school— football, basketball, swimming, track. Each fall he'd start off OK but then something would fuck him up—one season it was bronchitis, one season a sprained ankle, poor grades, academic probation, he'd get discouraged and smoke too much dope with his non-athlete friends so the coach had no choice but to drop him from the team.

His parents nagging him *When will you take responsibility for your life Bart—you are not a child any longer!*

His problem was, he'd been born the wrong color. If he'd been dark-skinned, some kind of slant-eyed Asian. Better yet, some kind of Native American. He'd be treated with respect not the way he was, treated like shit by his own parents. He could be *himself* and *himself* would be plenty.

He made a terrific first impression. Everybody said so.

Girls liked him—a lot. Then, if he was drinking, or high, or telling funny stories like the guys encouraged him, they'd kind of edge away and wouldn't want to see him a second time. That was the problem.

Every Delt-Sig party had been a fuck-up. Except freshman year a few times, the girls had been so young and naive and grateful for a guy to notice them, that'd been great. But then, things got fucked-up at homecoming, sophomore year. He never did figure out what the fuck had happened, he'd been too wasted.

THE EXECUTION

Bart Hansen hadn't been the only guy this "Kima Klausen" had identified to the dean. The way his parents ranted about it, you'd have thought he *was*.

Since the age of nine he'd suffered panic attacks. He'd looked like a healthy—husky—kid but the medical fact is, he's susceptible to "wild swings of mood"—this would be Deekman's defense.

Upper-middle-class suburban parents instilled in their adolescent son a continuous state of nerves, anxiety, a feeling of being *not good enough* Like so many other young people today in the United States he'd had to resort to self-medication for survival.

Self-medicating—just pot at first, in middle school, then stronger drugs, lots of drugs. And alcohol.

They'd kept him on a short leash like one of those pathetic little overbred dogs—jerking the leash anytime they wanted. He'd complained to his friends, bitter and aggrieved.

Years he'd been complaining. Since seventh grade at least.

Amber Bendemann would testify at the trial nobody thought Bart was serious! *Invasion of the Body Snatchers* he'd call it—*he* was the body snatcher and his parents were the bodies.

I mean, like, if somebody really wanted to murder his parents would he talk about it so much? In the school cafeteria?

Amber has this whiny little-girl voice, when she uttered these words there was laughter in the courtroom and even among the jurors, and the judge said sternly *Quiet! There is nothing remotely amusing about these proceedings.*

Bart had pleaded *not guilty* of course.

139

Though there was a possibility you could argue *self-defense*.

It was far-fetched and tricky but the fact was, Laurence Hansen was a tall burly quick-tempered man outweighing his son by at least twenty pounds; if he'd been struck down by his son, Bart had to have done it in self-defense.

Obviously Bart's father had heard him come into the house. Had heard someone enter the house, through the garage. He'd been hiding in wait for the intruder, behind the bedroom door. It was misleading to claim that the father had been struck down helpless in bed, on his back.

Luckily, Laurence Hansen hadn't owned a handgun. Maybe he'd assumed that the Vector Security alarm was all that he needed to protect himself and his family.

What had freaked Bart out—his father bellowing like a wounded calf. Lying in wait for him behind the door, and grabbing the door to open it as Bart pushed it stealthily open, and once he'd seen who the intruder was, once he'd identified Bart, and saw the ax in Bart's hands, what his failure as a parent was going to cost him, the man was doomed: for there was, for the vengeful ax, no turning back.

Like a kamikaze pilot. Their fuel was enough to get them to the target, not enough to return them back to the base. Once taken off in their kamikaze planes with the rising-sun insignia on the wings the young Japanese pilots could never return.

He'd seen a documentary on the kamikazes, on TV. Actual film footage of some of the pilots, the planes. Like brothers they were, so young, except they were Japs. And so long dead, it was like another world.

He'd have given his life for some great cause. *He'd* been born at the wrong time.

Materialist sleaze decade 1990s, he'd been a young kid. You never shake off the toxins of your psychic environment.

All his generation. Like, accursed.

Second semester senior year at Rensselaer Day he'd spent in a dope haze with his friends. They'd taken SATs, they'd gotten their university acceptances/rejections, it was easy sledding downhill from there. He'd felt pretty good about Syracuse, the Sigma Nu chapter was a popular frat house on the Hill, his dad was Sigma Nu from the University of Michigan so he'd thought it would be a breeze getting pledged there but it had not worked out that way.

Rush week had been a stark shitty time for him. You could say, he'd never recovered from rush week freshman year.

So he'd pledged Delt-Sig. The guys had made him feel welcome. The guys had made him feel they needed *him*.

The other fraternities hadn't been impressed with Bart, much. There was a lot of high-pressure competition.

Just Delt-Sig and two other fraternities, one of them on academic probation, had sent Bart Hansen bids.

He'd gotten drunk. He'd gotten shit-faced falling-down drunk. Fuck Sigma Nu, fuck Deke, fuck the Beta Gams. He wouldn't have pledged the fuckers if they'd begged him.

Laurence Hansen had been Sigma Nu, University of Michigan '80. It was a stunning surprise how the Syracuse chapter hadn't given a shit for the Hansen legacy though Laurence Hansen had given the fraternity money—Bart had reason to believe no less than five thousand dollars over all.

Start of rush week he'd thought—every freshman in his residence had thought—the Delt-Sigs were a bunch of losers, less than thirty actives living in the sprawling old Victorian house on Stadium Drive that looked like it had survived an A-bomb testing—like the outside paint had been leached of all color and inside on the walls you'd see the ghost-silhouettes of people who'd been vaporized into the wall and there was a rumor—(a rumor that turned out to be fact)—that the property was double-mortgaged and could be foreclosed anytime. On the inside walls in fact were framed group photos of Delt-Sigs from previous years—decades ago—three times as many members, and looking pretty good; in 1957 for instance the Delt-Sigs had had *four rowers on the crew team* that had competed in the national finals and come in third place, and 1966–68 they'd had half the S.U. track team and a star diver who'd gone on to compete in the U.S. Olympics; there were Delt-Sig alums who were state congressmen and at least one U.S. congressman, of which the fraternity was proud. In more recent years it looked as if the fraternity had had "challenges"—why this was, no one seemed to know. But the Delt-Sigs Bart had talked with, the Delt-Sigs who'd talked with him, at rush, had been really nice to him, and funny, and interesting—turned out, they liked the music

Bart liked, and video games, and TV programs, and shared his opinions about politics and lots of other things—they'd made Bart feel *like he mattered.*

So it turned out, pledging Delta Sigma meant more to Bart than he'd ever have expected. Telling his father he didn't give a fuck for Sigma Nu, he wouldn't accept a bid from Sigma Nu now, all that was finished. His mother knew, and sympathized. Telling him not to feel bad about his father's fraternity, just to make his own friends and forget the past.

So it was like she double-crossed him, a year later—two years later—siding with his father saying *If the fraternity drains so much of your time and money we can't afford, and there are drinking parties every weekend, maybe it would be better if—*

—maybe a better use of your time for studying, a better use of your money for tuition—

—your father can get you a summer internship he thinks at Squibb—

You'd think they would've supported him—his own parents! It had meant so much to Bart to be re-admitted to the university.

God damned university takes your money for the semester and *does not refund.*

Sophomore year he'd gotten into trouble and had been placed on "suspension"—he'd returned home and enrolled in Rensselaer Community College a mile from the house, computer science, accounting, and economics. At the start of the semester things were OK, he missed the Delt-Sigs like hell but was attending classes and impressing his instructors, then somehow, who knows how, he'd gotten bored, missed classes, and hung out with his high school buddies smoking dope like old times so he'd blown all three of the courses he might've gotten A's in—this was Rensselaer Community College for Christ's sake, this was not Syracuse University!—so had to make some arrangements with a guy he knew, he'd gotten introduced to, who could provide him with transcripts from the registrar he could forge, gave himself A's in computer science and accounting and a B+ in economics, which he figured he'd have gotten in any case if the semester had gone normally; and the surprise was—the dean's office at S.U. informed him that he was being "reinstated."

This was awesome! His father and mother had been impressed and proud of him.

He'd been, like, proud of himself for once. Not made to feel like he was utter shit and looked down upon by the world.

Still he's pissed: forty-three thousand a year and if you flunk courses, or get incompletes, it's money down the toilet—just *gone.* He's made to feel ashamed, he isn't technically a "junior" like his friends. (He might not graduate with his class, if things don't improve. He might not graduate!)

The fraternity is on his ass, too. Not his friends but the God-damned Delta Sigma Corporation, it's called.

To be re-activated in Delta Sigma you must repay all outstanding loans as well as a good-faith deposit of $1,500 for 2012.

He's insulted. He tries not to think of it. Though he was initiated into Delta Sigma he knows there are guys in the fraternity who never accepted him—only just voted to admit him because the chapter needs members, it's in danger of going off-campus.

But mostly he's crazy for the fraternity. His only friends in the world are Delt-Sigs. He wears the little gold lapel pin in the (secret) shape of an Egyptian scarab, he's proud of. Jesus, he'd die for those guys.

Which is why he was so astonished, deeply wounded, and mortified in his soul, to learn that several Delt-Sigs betrayed him to the Rensselaer police.

In secret the police had "interviewed" every guy in the fraternity. In secret, at grand jury hearings Bart's lawyer Davis Deekman hadn't been allowed to attend, at least six of Bart's frat brothers gave statements that must've incriminated him, for the jury had handed down an indictment—*one count of homicide in the second degree, one count of aggravated assault with the intent to commit homicide, in the first degree.*

Bart's account was, he'd remained at the Delt-Sig house all night. Lots of guys had seen him. He'd slept on the sofa in the basement in that room that's a kind of no-man's-land where spare furniture is kept, just lay on the old worn brown leather sofa and slept, and didn't wake up until about 8 A.M.—came upstairs into the kitchen at about 8:30 A.M. for breakfast.

(There's no formal breakfast at Delt-Sig, just breakfast supplies you help yourself to.)

Obviously, Bart had been at the frat house all night. Guys would testify to this, they'd seen him at about midnight, or later, upstairs; he'd gone downstairs to crash; then, in the morning, they saw him again, and would provide him with an alibi for the night—it was the least he could expect of them and he'd been fucked, he'd never felt so betrayed, when at least three of the guys, the guys he'd been counting on, broke down when the detectives interviewed them saying that they hadn't seen Bart except before about 1 A.M. and after 8 A.M.

His brain just shuts off. Thinking of this enormity is like trying to shove some outsized object like a tennis racket into a small space like the inside of his skull.

It was a weird story like something on TV. Trying to comprehend it Bart has the idea it is something he'd actually seen on TV but not recently, when he'd been a little kid maybe.

All he knew was, he'd wakened in the frat house. He'd come upstairs and talked with the guys, he was feeling kind of excitable and high since he'd had a good night's sleep, only a mild headache from the beer of the previous night, and some heartburn from the pizza, but he was feeling really good, and thinking of going to some of his old classes just to sit at the back of the lecture hall, to show his serious intentions, though he hadn't actually gone—and next thing he knew, at about noon, the first sign that things were fucked-up, a reporter for the Syracuse newspaper came to the frat house, bulled his way inside and asked if "Bart Harrison"—"who lives in East Rensselaer"—was on the premises; and one of the guys went to find Bart, and Bart swallowed hard and was following him back, just knowing this had to be some kind of bummer, and it was at that moment that the Rensselaer PD cruiser pulled up outside the frat house at about thirty miles an hour and conspicuously braked to a stop. And nothing was ever the same again.

Jesus! Like the earth opened, and I fell inside.

And just fell and fell and fell. . . .

He'd been so surprised. So shocked. He hadn't been able to comprehend what the police officers were telling him at first.

His father's death—"murder."

His mother, severely injured, in a coma in the Rensselaer hospital—"in critical condition."

Crudely the police officers revealed this terrible news. Crudely and coldly eyeing the Hansens' twenty-year-old son Bart with scarcely concealed contempt and Bart had not—had not comprehended—so stunned, the roaring in his ears so distracting, he hadn't comprehended what any of them were telling him out of earshot of the Delt-Sigs somberly gathered in the front hall of the frat house—hadn't fully comprehended the news—for he'd believed he had heard—he was certain, he'd heard   that they'd informed him that both his parents were dead—Louisa and Laurence, both dead—murdered. He'd been utterly surprised. Eyes widened, and tears welling in his eyes—hyperventilating and beginning to bawl like a baby so—shocked.

My—parents? Somebody killed my—parents?

My mom? My dad?

He'd been panicked, he would be required to identify the bodies.

His father! His mother! His—*mother.*

He'd bawled like a baby mashing his fists into his eyes.

He'd had to sit down. The elasticized waistband of his jockey shorts cutting into his skin in that way he hated, and a hot smell of his body wafting from him to the detectives' nostrils judging from their expressions, a bad smell.

My parents! My parents are—dead. . . .

I don't believe it! It can't be real!

I just t-talked to them the other—yesterday morning—they wanted me to come home this weekend but I, I—I explained to them—

The police officers were quiet, regarding him. In their eyes he saw no sympathy, which was shocking to him, unnerving.

He hadn't been prepared for the astonishment to come.

They were telling him his mother was not dead but alive.

His father was dead. His father had been murdered.

His mother had been severely injured, yet was not dead but alive.

Do you think that your mother is dead, Bart? Why do you think that your mother is dead?

Stammering *That—that's what you told me. You told me—oh God—my p-parents were dead. But—*

No, Bart. Your mother is not dead. Your mother is in a coma.

C-Coma . . .

But before she lost consciousness she named you, Bart. Your mother named you as the person who had attacked her and had murdered your father, that's you, Bart.

This, Bart truly could not comprehend. This had to be totally impossible, the cops were lying to him.

In someplace confusing to him he was sitting—the strength had drained out of his knees, he'd had to sit down. He saw how the police officers who were plainclothes were flanking him, one to his right, one to his left, and the lead detective, whose name he'd immediately forgotten, was questioning him like he already knew every answer Bart could give. This was—such a shock! His heart was pounding like a fist against his rib cage, he was hyperventilating and the cops didn't give a damn, didn't even notice—his mom would have noticed, and tried to comfort him.

They were saying—what? His mother was in a coma. His mother *was not dead.*

See, Bart: she named you. Your mother named you as the assail-ant. When the medics came to your house and the first police officers arrived your mother was still conscious though she'd lost a lot of blood, and so she was asked by one of our officers Do you know who did this to you, Mrs. Hansen? *and though she couldn't speak she was able to nod her head, yes; and she was asked, "Was the assailant someone in your family?" and she was able to nod her head, yes; and she was asked, "Was the assailant your son?"—(the officer was guessing, your parents would have at least one son)—and she seemed to be nodding, yes. And she passed out then and they took her away.*

They were arresting him! Hadn't come to the Delta Sigma house to break the terrible news of his parents' deaths but were callously *arresting him.*

The Delt-Sigs were looking on as Bart was half-led, half-carried out to the PD cruiser—all the guys, astonished. *What the fuck? What is this? What're they doing to Bart?* And out on the front walk gaping like he's a freak show asshole, Theta Pis from next door, and two girls—gorgeous girls—from the Chi Omega house, Oh Christ!—all gaping at *him*.

That night, 10 P.M. DeMarco Pizza delivery van rolls up, doorbell rings and it's eight large pizzas for the Delt-Sigs—this is all that Bart had gotten around to ordering but a nice surprise for his frat brothers, after this nightmare day that has left them stunned—"freaked"—and there's local TV news footage of the shabby exterior of the Delt-Sig house and guys on the front stoop shouting obscenities and giving reporters the finger—not such a great image for the fraternity.

Deekman, Davis. His dad's golf-club friend who was the kind of lawyer Bart needed: criminal defense.

Not that Dad had ever been a really close friend of Deekman, he'd complained that Deekman cheated at golf when he could get away with it. But Davis Deekman was the only name Bart knew, and Deekman would know *him*.

As it turned out, Deekman was a terrific choice.

One of the first things Deekman did was arrange for Bart's Explorer to be driven back to East Rensselaer, for safekeeping.

And he'd tried to get Bart out of the crummy detention facility, tried to arrange for bail, but even an exorbitant bail was denied for Bart Hansen was considered a *flight risk*.

It was like a terrible joke, Bart would protest to friends. He's devastated his parents have been murdered and all the cops and the judge can think of is—he's a *fucking flight risk*.

Swiftly too much was happening. Great stretches of Bart's life so F U C K I N G B O R I N G it was like he'd been crawling on hands and knees through the Sahara Desert in slow-motion but now suddenly, when he's weak, and emotionally fragile, everything is speeded-up like—like the world is on crystal meth and he's the only sane one.

His mind *goes blank*. Starts to think of the situation he's in and the terrible fact that his parents are dead. . . . The realization hits him in the gut like he's been kicked, his insides are churning with a need to use the toilet, fast—nobody gives a damn how sick he is, how clammy-cold his skin is— that he's having a full-fledged panic attack and could die.

One good thing: he'd decided better not look for his father's wallet in the bedroom, remove bills and credit cards like the Visa Platinum the way a burglar would. For now the cops would've discovered Laurence Hansen's credit cards in Bart's possession and how'd Bart explain *that?*

Relatives come to see him in the Rensselaer County Detention Center where he's in "isolation" and he tells them that it is not true—it is a lie—that his mother *identified him* as the assailant: "That is just not possible. I was not there!" He has no idea who killed his parents—that is, his father—he guesses it had to have been a break-in, a "home invasion"—like that one in Connecticut a couple of years ago—and his father had defied the intruders, and was killed for his courage. And his mother . . .

Well, the fact is—Bart has to keep reminding himself—his mother is *alive*. Bart's mother is not dead like his father but *in a coma*.

The relatives are praying for Louisa. Neighbors, friends. All are praying for Louisa Hansen to recover from her terrible injuries.

Bart, too. Of course, Bart is praying, too. Tearful Bart asks to be allowed to visit his mother in the Rensselaer hospital but his request is denied.

Bart tells anyone who will listen that he knows nothing about the ax attack. He'd been at the frat house in Syracuse all that night—his frat brothers will vouch for him. In fact, he'd been in Syracuse for all of that week. He'd talked with his parents only a few days before and there had been "no sign" of anything wrong, he was sure.

His dad had enemies, he believed. Business enemies. And the house on Juniper Drive is "kind of a 'conspicuous consumption' house"—(he'd gotten this fancy term from his S.U. economics prof)—somebody'd be led to think whoever lived there had *money*.

Rensselaer County prosecutors were suggesting that the ax attack had been perpetrated for motives of money: the son, deeply in debt, having forged his father's signature on a $28,000 check the previous December to pay for a new SUV, and in arrears with his fraternity, was counting on life-insurance money coming to him, as well as his parents' estate—estimated at approximately three million dollars.

Three million! Bart had had the idea that his parents were worth a lot more than that—ten million at least. The way the old man *hinted* and *boasted*.

What about the property in Bolton Landing? Bart's father's family had owned it for, like, generations—a sprawling old Adirondack lodge on three acres overlooking Lake George. Wasn't that worth a couple million dollars, at least?

The life-insurance policies weren't great but OK: two hundred thousand on Laurence's life, sixty thousand on Louisa's life. You had to figure the mother's life was worth less because she didn't have an income like the father.

Bart finds it difficult to comprehend, he isn't going to receive this money. He is his parents' beneficiary but only if both are deceased; the situation being what it is, and Louisa still alive, she is Laurence's beneficiary and twenty-year-old Bart doesn't get a dime.

Rensselaer County prosecutors had confiscated both the Hansens' personal computers as well as Bart's personal computer and were concocting a narrative of *vengeful, calculating, murderous son* on the spurious evidence of e-mail communications between parents and son over a period of eighteen months, the forged check for the down payment on the Explorer, e-mail exchanges with the Sigma Nu Corporation, and reported conversations with friends of the defendant.

In the face of this *mounting suspicion,* as the media described it, Deekman was cool and efficient. He didn't waste words and didn't allow his client to waste words either. Often when Bart began to speak to him in a loud aggrieved voice he lifted a hand to signal *No more.* (Their meetings were held in an allegedly soundproof room at the detention center. But anyone who believed that the prosecution wasn't spying on them, Deekman said, didn't need a lawyer but a psychiatrist.)

When Bart started to explain to him another time how he'd been at the Delt-Sig house all that night when his parents were killed Deekman lifted his hand saying curtly *Understood.*

Yet, despite Deekman's efforts, they'd indicted Bart Hansen. The Rensselaer prosecutors who seemed to have no one to vent their spite upon, no object or target for their vituperation except the bereft son of murdered parents—(that is, one murdered parent and the other comatose)—triumphed in the courthouse and in the local media.

RENSSELAER YOUTH, 20, INDICTED IN MURDER OF FATHER
ATTEMPTED MURDER OF MOTHER
MOTHER IDENTIFIES SON BEFORE LAPSING INTO COMA

In all of upstate New York TV news and newspapers—and online—it was repeated again and again—again—that the *severely injured mother had managed to identify her son before lapsing into a coma;* and the issue was, would such an accusation be allowed in a trial, if there was a trial? If the mother did not wake from the coma, to repeat her statement in court, or—if the mother died . . .

Deekman was adamant: if there was a trial it could not be held in Rensselaer County or anywhere near. Nowhere in this part of New York State where the media have shamelessly exploited his client's personal tragedy.

In the Rensselaer hospital, Louisa Hansen remains *in a comatose state, on life-support machines.*

In the Rensselaer County detention facility, Bart Hansen remains in custody awaiting trial, kept apart from other inmates.

In Bart's lower gut there is a ceaseless churning of anxiety, misery. Gas pains like knife stabs coming one-two-three so he practically faints sometimes. Yet, he has not lost weight in this terrible environment— he has actually gained weight around his middle, flabby-doughy flesh the hue of Wonder Bread. Made to walk around—"exercise"—in what passes for a gym in the dank interior of the facility—he becomes quickly short of breath.

Why Bart is kept isolated from other inmates in the detention center he isn't certain. Not just the color of his skin—there are a few other white men in the facility he has noticed, or what you'd describe as "white."

Mostly dark-skinned men and boys staring at him as he's led past their cells to his own at the far end of a corridor. Lucky they can't get close to him, all they can do is bare their teeth at him *Hey white boy. Yo fuckin fag you kill you momma asshole?*

Even the guards are disdainful of Bart Hansen. White guys, dark-skinned. Never call him by any name except *you* or maybe, if he's slow to move, *You, Ha'sen.*

Alone, Bart watches TV. Crummy small-screen TV and no cable. His jaws clench, his back teeth grind. He is incredulous!

Can't believe his frat-brothers testified *against him* at the grand jury hearing.

The "identification" of Bart his mother allegedly made, prominently featured in all media accounts of the ax attack, Bart scarcely considers at all. First, he can't and won't believe it for he knows that his mother adores him and though she might be pissed with him sometimes, she'd never wish to seriously harm *him;* the cop must've tricked her into nodding her head or the cop made it all up—none of it had happened. Deekman is fighting to exclude the "so-called identification" from evidence to be presented at the trial; particularly, he is adamant that the "hearsay evidence" provided by the medics at the scene will be excluded.

All this while—weeks, months!—briefs are being filed. Petitions to the court. Deekman is demanding a change of venue. Bart's relatives have ceased to visit him. His dad's older brother, his aunt Sheila who's a high school teacher in Elmira—they'd seemed sympathetic with Bart at the start, now less so. The Delt-Sigs he'd been closest to have never come to visit him—not once.

The soberng fact is—except for his mother nobody gives a damn whether Bart Hansen lives or dies.

If he'd had a girlfriend. A loyal girlfriend to have faith in him and visit him in detention; to come to his trial and sit conspicuously behind him, for the gawkers to see—that would impress the jury.

Sometimes, a juror will fall in love with a defendant. Bart seems to recall that that happened with Ted Bundy the notorious

serial killer, when he was defending himself in a Florida courtroom, and maybe with Robert Chambers, the "preppy" murderer
in New York City.

His father's life-insurance policy will pay $200,000 to Louisa
Hansen, not to Bart; for Bart is not the "surviving" son and can
make no claim so long as his mother is alive. And his father's
"estate"—whatever that includes—continues to belong to his
mother, so long as she is alive. Bart asks Deekman could he
take out a loan against the life insurance and/or the estate he
will inherit—(he assumes he will inherit, he has not actually
seen his parents' wills)—and Deekman counsels him no, this
is probably not a good idea for Bart must keep in mind that he
has had a "negative" press and people are "prejudiced" against
him, that's the problem.

One of the problems.

Innocent till proven guilty—that was a laugh.

Bart is thinking: he will go on TV talk shows, when this fiasco
is ended. He will *plead his case to the American public and see who
they believe!*

Here was good news: the judge granted the defense a change
of venue for the trial, to Niagara County in western New York
State, due to the "extensive and protracted" publicity accruing
to the case in the Rensselaer-Albany area.

This was a triumph for Deekman. And it was a triumph for
Deekman that the statements of two medics who'd claimed to
have "witnessed" Louisa Hansen identify her son as her assailant
at the crime scene would not be admissible in court.

Deekman said, not a chance the prosecution can convince a jury, all they have is circumstantial evidence not physical evidence.

Physical evidence meant fingerprints for instance.

Physical evidence meant bloodstains on clothing known to be Bart Hansen's clothing not merely the Hansens' bloodstains on clothing retrieved from a reeking Dumpster at a rest stop at exit 19, New York Thruway (east) that were "so generic" they could belong to anyone.

The assailant's clothing, evidently. This was indisputable. But that the clothing was Bart Hansen's was not so easy to confirm, as Deekman would brilliantly argue.

Months later at the trial—in Niagara County, in western New York State—the bloodstained clothing would be a hotly contested issue. No prosecution witness could claim that the bloodstained clothes were definitely Bart Hansen's—or maybe just looked like clothes Bart wore.

Kind of, like, a heavy-metal influence—except Bart didn't have tattoos or piercings.

As, at the trial, when the Delt-Sigs took the witness stand to testify—in suits, dress shirts, and ties, clean-shaven and abashed, unable to bring themselves to look at their frat brother Bart Hansen quivering with indignation at the defense table—it would turn out that, closely questioned by Davis Deekman, not one of the frat boys could *absolutely claim that Bart Hansen hadn't been in the fraternity house through the night of April 11, only that they hadn't seen him between the hours of 1 A.M. and approximately 8:30 A.M.*

As to the E-ZPass "evidence"—and the claim of a Juniper Drive neighbor that he'd seen Bart's Explorer in the driveway of the Hansens' house at about the time of the attack—Deekman offered an explanation that was, if not entirely plausible, yet not entirely implausible: that another individual, unknown to Bart Hansen, or perhaps known to him, had taken the Explorer while he was sleeping in the frat house, driven three hours and twenty minutes to East Rensselaer to break into the Hansens' house, having heard that Bart Hansen's family was well-to-do, and committed the terrible crimes—all while Bart was sleeping oblivious.

This may be one of the most ingeniously planned and staged crimes of our time—it may be revealed, my client is as much a victim as his parents!

Then, the most astonishing reversal: Louisa Hansen, the prosecution's leading witness, had changed her mind about accusing her son.

Far from identifying Bart as the individual who'd killed her husband and had tried to kill her, Mrs. Hansen was now claiming that she remembered nothing of the assault; and that she could not have said what police officers were claiming she'd said—*That is ridiculous. I never saw his face.*

The badly injured and mutilated woman had regained consciousness after nearly twenty days in a comatose state but for some time afterward her condition was so grave, her ability to comprehend and to communicate so limited, no one from the Rensselaer County prosecutor's office was allowed to meet with her.

During these weeks Mrs. Hansen underwent a number of surgeries—neuro, ophthalmologic, dental, cosmetic; she had surgery to repair a near-severed tendon in her left leg, and she had gastrointestinal procedures to correct inflammations and abscesses in her large colon. She was fed intravenously. She began to regain some of the weight she'd so drastically lost and gradually, with the purposeful air of one struggling to haul herself out of a murky sea, she began to regain a fuller consciousness, and a memory.

Five months after the ax attack it began to be rumored in courthouse circles and in the media that *the murderer's mother* was changing her statement; the following week, a gloating Davis Deekman called a press conference to announce that Louisa Hansen was "not only repudiating her accusation of her son" but would be the defense's "leading witness" in the upcoming trial.

Crude tabloid headlines trumpeted this reversal, a terrible blow to the prosecution: BART'S MOM CLAIMS: "MY SON IS NOT A MURDERER."

And, BRAIN-INJURED MOM-VICTIM CLAIMS: "NOT MY SON!"

Louisa Hansen was insisting now that she could not remember anything of the assault, or almost anything; she could remember nothing of what followed when the Rensselaer police officer allegedly questioned her in the bedroom. She had a "vague, confused" memory of being lifted onto a stretcher, and being strapped down and carried away. She may have had a "blurred" memory of a siren, an ambulance ride, a hospital. But she did not remember seeing her husband—her husband's body. And definitely, she *did not remember seeing her son in her bedroom, with an ax.*

To refute the prosecution's initial claim that Louisa Hansen could have identified her son as the assailant, given her physical injuries at the time, Deekman had enlisted a battery of expert witnesses to present to the court—a neurologist, a neuroscientist whose specialty was vision, a psychiatrist, a cognitive psychologist, even a family therapist whom Louisa had seen intermittently in Rensselaer: for how could so severely traumatized an individual, her skull smashed and scalp bleeding profusely, one eye hanging from its socket, lacerations and deep wounds on many parts of her body, obviously in shock, and, seven hours after the attack, weak from loss of blood, possibly have comprehended any question put to her, let alone answered it accurately? Now, Louisa Hansen herself would be refuting the prosecution's claim: the testimony by the police officer who'd allegedly asked her if "her son" had hurt her and her husband. Without the medics' testimonies to bolster his, the police officer did not appear so convincing, cross-examined by Davis Deekman. For he, too, would have been "shaken and distracted" by so horrific a crime scene and could not possibly remember all that had passed between him and the injured woman.

Initially, Louisa Hansen had said that she was sure that Bart had nothing to do with the attack: she *would know* if he had—she was his mother after all. She *would know*.

Then, as she regained strength, and her voice, Louisa began to insist that she had not ever identified her son as her assailant: that this was an "outright lie."

She had no memory of that night—or, the vaguest memory.

Things had passed in a "blur"—"like a dream"—yet she was sure that Bart had not been "anywhere near" the house that night.

At the trial, testifying on behalf of her son, Louisa Hansen spoke haltingly but forcefully as everyone in the courtroom stared at her; and no one more avidly than Bart Hansen.

Louisa said she didn't know if she'd dreamt—something. She knew that her brain had been injured and she'd had neurosurgeries and had been unconscious and conscious and unconscious and "floating" with painkillers—but sometimes things were sharp, what was cloudy became clear like a smudged glass that was polished, and so she thought now she could remember—she *did remember*—a human figure, a man, a "stranger"—she'd had an impression of a "swarthy" skin—a "creased" face—a "not-young" face; he'd had that kind of beard that's trimmed short—"I think it's called a—goatee."

Carefully Deekman summarized: "Your assailant, Mrs. Hansen, was a 'swarthy-skinned' man, 'not-young,' with a 'creased' face and a 'goatee'? No one you recognized?"

"I think so. Yes. Or it might have been a . . ."

Louisa's single, occluded eye shifted in its socket, as if with effort. Her sunken mouth was fixed in a small determined smile of the kind intended to assure others, *I am all right, I am fine: don't worry about me!* despite her ravaged face and slight, broken body. She was peering past the aggressive Deekman at her son Bart who sat at the defense table not fifteen feet away with hunched shoulders, an abashed and stricken look on his face. Bart's youth was fading, even his dun-colored limp hair appeared thin at the crown. His skin had become puffy and sallow as if water bloated. His eyes formerly quick, elusive, and sly as small fish darting in a pond were puffy, too, and chronically ringed in fatigue. Yet on Bart's lips, too, there appeared a faint hopeful smile.

Son and mother had seen little of each other in the intervening eleven months.

". . . might have been a dream. I can't be sure."

"But you are sure, Mrs. Hansen, that you didn't see *your son Bart* in your bedroom that night?"

"Oh yes. I am sure of that. I didn't see my son Bart in my —our—bedroom that night. The intruder was a—*stranger.*"

Louisa's right eye had been surgically removed and had not yet been replaced with an artificial eye: the socket was empty, but resembled melted wax, and was not deep. Her skull and facial bones had been smashed and had not quite healed, appearing re-aligned, mismatched; her nose had been mashed and flattened; her skin was scarred and ravaged and her mouth shrunken, for her lower jaw had been badly lacerated; most of her teeth had been lost, and she'd been fitted with an abbreviated set of artificial teeth. Her hair, shaved for surgery, had grown back thinly, and was ghostly white. Yet relatives and friends of Louisa Hansen claimed that within the mutilated face you could see the former face of Louisa Hansen, unmistakably.

The poor woman's body appeared broken, her spine hunched and her head pushed forward; she walked with difficulty, using a cane, needing assistance, yet there was an air of resilience and even defiance about her, that made her a powerfully appealing figure. For her courtroom appearance Mrs. Hansen had dressed herself, or had been dressed, in a way to suggest understated good taste, a dark mulberry pants suit, a white silk blouse, a strand of pearls and matching earrings.

In the Rensselaer-Albany area there was intense, intrusive interest in the "murderer's mother"—in Niagara County, hundreds of miles to the west, there was a sympathetic if somewhat morbid interest in the "mother of the defendant": Louisa Hansen's bravery, her composure. For Louisa was a widow, too—she'd lost her husband, as she had nearly lost her own life. Yet she seemed totally *without bitterness or reproach.*

She'd described herself as *A Christian woman. That is my family heritage, and it is my son's heritage, too.*

Bart wiped at his eyes with his fists. Oh Christ now he would cry! Crying was a sign of guilt, remorse. *He would not cry.*

He was sulky, sullen. He'd been humiliated, plenty—his frat brothers had let him down publicly. No girl would ever go out with him on the S.U. campus even if he was fully reinstated. Unflattering photographs of him had appeared in print, on TV, and online—he'd have liked to protest *That is not me! That is not me God damn you.*

Why the Delt-Sigs had caved and testified for the prosecution, Deekman had explained: they'd been threatened with *aiding and abetting a crime* and *obfuscation of justice* if they'd supported Bart's alibi and it had turned out that Bart was found guilty of the crime.

Hadn't had faith in him, that was the point.

At least his mother was on his side. Finally!

Her—she'd caused all this. She'd let him down. She'd reneged on promises she'd made to him, many times. She'd cared more for her God damn garden-club friends than she ever had for *him*.

In the flower beds about the house, those tall showy neon-orange flowers—gladioli? Weird *vertical* flowers that had to be propped up or they'd fall over in a rainstorm.

Still, Louisa Hansen's flowers were impressive. Classy, eye-catching. His mom was some kind of star in the Rensselaer Women's Garden Club—he'd seen her photo in the local newspaper —that meant a lot to her.

He hadn't even realized that she was forty-six years old!—until it was mentioned in the media. And his father, fifty-one.

So *old*. Bart intends to never wind up so *old*.

Seeing their pictures was weird. The first thing you think, why'd anybody care enough about Dad to print his picture in the paper? Or Mom?

The grotesque melted face, the faltering voice, the single re-cessed eye and the way her slight body was collapsed into the witness chair like a discarded puppet—all this seemed to assure the courtroom that Louisa Hansen was telling the truth. Where her testimony differed from the testimonies of others, it was those others who were mistaken, or lying, and not her. In fact, after Louisa Hansen's testimony it was difficult to recall others who'd preceded her.

Until now, the trial had passed, for Bart, in a toxic haze. To save his sanity he'd had to let his mind wander. Shoot up with something like Novocain. Hadn't smoked pot in such a long God damned time, he tried to recall the sensation, that was soothing. Comforting. And the beer buzz at the back of his head, Christ he missed *that*. Ritalin and any uppers he didn't want, fuck no. Just needed to be calm—like, meditate. Sat at the defense table with his arms folded tight across his chest, trying not to wince with intestinal pain. *Try not to scowl* he'd been advised by Deekman. Fuck he wasn't *scowling*!

Continually outside the courtroom Deekman is asked: Will your client take the stand? Testify in his own defense?

Deekman is courteous, deadpan *No*.

No? And why not?

Which part of the word don't you understand? N—O. NO.

Bart is thinking he should testify—people think you're guilty if you don't. But Deekman won't even discuss the issue with him. And frankly Bart is relieved, he's seen how witnesses who start out confident can get tripped up, make fools of themselves, or appear to be deceitful when questioned by a shrewd and (it seems) conscienceless attorney. Like the police officer who'd claimed to "question" Louisa Hansen despite her terrible injuries—who'd claimed that Louisa had actually *nodded her head* in response to his questions—Deekman had made an asshole of the guy in just a few words.

How Deekman did it is a mystery! Bart has to concede, you wouldn't want this guy on the other side.

Five hundred bucks an hour, minimum. Plus there's a "defense team"—a half-dozen younger assistants, looks like.

Bart had said he wasn't sure if he could pay him—or when. Deekman laid a hand on his shoulder like Bart Hansen was his own son saying *My fee is not an issue. Getting you free is.*

Bart tells himself that when this fiasco is over, and his real life resumes—he'll see an adviser at the university to plan a pre-law major.

Corporate law. Sports-injury law. Those guys raked in dough!

Criminal defense law, he didn't think he could master. Not like Davis Deekman. You had to be quick-witted and kind of duplicitous—tricky. It was something like playing chess if you could find a way to guide your opponent's hand, too—force him to move a chess piece in a way not to his advantage.

Bart was grateful to Deekman, though, for showing him a way to see how the ax attack might've occurred without Bart being involved. It *was* possible—some other individual, maybe a Delt-Sig, driving to East Rensselaer, etcetera. *Beyond a shadow of a doubt* was a sound principle.

After Bart's mother's testimony, no one else and nothing else seemed important in the trial. Bart's mother continued to attend the trial, seated just behind the defense table. She dressed herself, or was dressed, in dark clothes like a woman in mourning, very tasteful, classy. She sat with relatives who took care of her, Bart was relieved to see.

She'd help him with the law school tuition. Anything to do with school, courses, self-improvement—she'd always encouraged him.

Dad had had the attitude—*Well sure. Let's give it a try*—so you could see he was skeptical, bemused, waiting for Bart to fuck up.

Why's it my fault, he'd wanted to demand of them, you didn't have more kids? *Superior* kids? Think if you'd had some other sons, they'd make you more proud than Bart did? Fuck it!

Had to laugh. Not once had his dad been *on his side*.

After five and a half weeks the trial ended. After jurors deliberated for seventy hours, a message came to the judge that the jury was "deadlocked."

Meaning that nine jurors had voted *guilty* while three had voted *not guilty*.

It only takes one. We will find that one. Deekman had not predicted he would find three!

What was—astonishing—almost unbelievable—was how immediately following the jury's decision, as the courtroom registered shock, and even the judge stared at him, Bart Hansen was a "free man."

Months he'd been kept in captivity like an animal, now he was *a free man*.

Bart went to his mother, seated behind the defense table. Bart stooped to embrace her and they wept together.

I love you, my darling baby, I love you. You are my darling darling baby I love you so.

I love you, too, Mom.

Now he would wish he hadn't told so many of the guys that he'd hated his parents. That if *something happened* they'd deserved it.

Well, that had been true of the old man. Not so true of his mother.

Mom I'm so sorry! Hey Mom I love you.

I know you do, Bart. I know you love me.

The prosecutors were poor losers. Threatening how they'd try Bart another time. Deekman assured him this would not happen. They had no way to circumnavigate Louisa Hansen's testimony—a new trial would end with another hung jury. *It only takes one.*

In the months following the trial the mother astounded many observers by giving interviews—print, TV. It was fascinating to see the fragile woman with the face that looked like melted wax, a single eye and sunken mouth, insisting that her son *had nothing to do with hurting her or with hurting his father.*

In a pleading voice she said *You would have to be this boy's mother to know him.*

There is a place in a child's soul only a mother can know.

She would be led to volunteer, drawn out by sympathetic-seeming interviewers on cable TV, that when she'd been a "young, immature mother" she'd taken tranquilizers and sleeping pills because motherhood had seemed "overwhelming" to her—she'd wanted to be a perfect mother and lost sight of the fact that *no one is perfect.*

So she believed she had lost her son for some years. From the time the child was five or six until—oh, maybe sixteen—or, maybe—to the present time. Not his fault but hers.

She wrote a letter to area newspapers claiming that the prosecutors of Rensselaer County had unjustly persecuted her son and never made the slightest attempt to find the actual murderer of her beloved husband. As if, if they couldn't blame her son, they had no interest in anyone else.

The letter was many times replicated in print and online.

> *I am pleading with you, the Prosecutor's Office of Rensselaer County, New York, to desist in harassing my son with threats of retrying him for a crime he did not commit and knew nothing of. I am begging you to allow us to get on with our lives after this catastrophe as we are trying to do.*
>
> *Sincerely, Louisa Hansen*

It was curious, Louisa Hansen rarely mentioned her late husband. It was as if the catastrophe that had happened, had happened to her and her son Bart alone.

The son escorted the mother to interviews. Sometimes the son consented to be interviewed with the mother though Davis Deekman strongly advised against this: for there was the possibility of a second trial, still.

The tabloid press and cable channels paid as much as $3,500 for an interview. There was a need for money: the two-hundred-thousand-dollar life-insurance policy paid to Louisa Hansen had gone for Bart's legal expenses, entirely; the house at 29 Juniper Drive had to be sold, below its market value, for the remainder of Deekman's bill, as well as for living expenses for the mother and son.

The Bolton Landing property, valued at one million dollars, had been on the market for months and few prospective buyers had seen it. The sprawling old Adirondack house was badly in need of repair, the dock on Lake George ravaged in storms, and the gravel driveway nearly washed away.

In the Village of East Rensselaer, Louisa and Bart Hansen have become a familiar pair. Mrs. Hansen has bought a two-bedroom condominium in a whitely shining new high-rise building in a residential neighborhood close by the First Episcopal Church and within easy commuting of Rensselaer Community College where Bart is enrolled in a degree-granting program in business administration. With her myriad disabilities, Louisa isn't able to drive: Bart drives her everywhere. The Explorer had to be sold and so Bart drives his father's sturdy dun-colored Lexus, taking his mother to her many medical appointments, to her hairdresser, to the Village library, to the First Episcopal Church of Rensselaer, to the homes of certain of her faithful friends, and to her several women's clubs.

Louisa says in interviews *I have no one but Bart now. I will devote my life to clearing my son's name.*

There have been those—Louisa's family, relatives, friends— who've tried to reason with her, to suggest that living with Bart might be dangerous, but Louisa cuts them off curtly. Ridiculous!

There is enough money to live on—just comfortably. Nothing like the multi-million-dollar estate Bart had naively anticipated. Joke's on him, Bart thinks! For it seems that Laurence Hansen died leaving behind questionable investments in discredited hedge funds, snarled finances. And he hadn't kept up repairs at the Bolton Landing house.

* * *

Bart blames the father for the mother's money worries—"He should have left you better taken care of, Mom. He always seemed to be boasting about that." Halfheartedly Louisa defends Laurence—"Well. Your father loved us. He just didn't always know how to show it. He was a *good man*"—and Bart says, humoring her, "Sure, Mom."

At church, the Hansens are often observed. Rarely do they miss a Sunday service. Their pew is fourth from the altar, facing the pulpit. Patiently Bart walks with his mother, who grips a cane in one hand and Bart's arm in the other: she is half his size, small and broken-backed, yet warmly friendly to all who greet them, and always very tastefully dressed in somber clothing. After church, Bart drives Louisa to the Women's Village Club, or to the Garden Club, for a lavish Sunday brunch. Bart is the only *son* in the gathering.

Eyes move on them, mesmerized.

Do you know who. Who they are?

What the son did . . .

No girl will come between them. No deceitful frat brothers.

He'd quit the fraternity for sure. Never again pledge any fucking fraternity in good faith, Bart has learned his lesson.

Still owes the Delta Sigma Corporation about one thousand dollars, with fines. Fuck you, sue me, Bart says.

His Rensselaer high school friends have mostly departed. He has friends numbering in the hundreds, online.

His names there are *Cloudsplitter, Hercules II, Sabbathblack, Hotdickke.* He has never arranged to meet anyone he has contacted online, however—how'd you trust any of them to be who they claim they are?

Just like the Delt-Sigs, probably. Lift any rock and what you see scuttling beneath—that's human nature, mostly.

He tries not to be cynical, though. At church, he sits beside his mother gazing at the minister's face, nodding, smiling, with a look of intense listening, rapport.

God forgives. It is not given to us to comprehend God's ways.

The only lengthy drive Bart is required to make with Louisa is to the medical center at the Albany Medical School. There, Louisa sees a neurologist whose specialty is impaired vision. For Louisa is losing vision in her single remaining eye and has been experiencing flashing lights, migraines. Louisa relates to Bart that her nightmare is of *something ugly and sharp* flying loose—like a rabid bat, except not a living thing.

"Yeh." Bart rubs his eyes with his fists, grunting. "Some weird-fuck thing like that, I dream of it, too."

Louisa stiffens. Bart realizes, he has misspoken.

"Hey I mean—yeh. Some weird thing like that."

Helping his mother out of the Lexus, at the entrance of the neurology clinic, while he drives into the high-rise parking garage to park. Then hurrying back to her as he sees her walking, trying to walk, toward the revolving-door entrance, leaning on her cane, faltering, as if determined to show that despite her infirmities, she can walk by herself. Bart comes up behind her—"Hey, Mom.

Wait. Let me get the—" It pisses him that she'd have plunged into the revolving door, the cane would get caught and she'd be knocked down or worse yet, dragged inside the door like some kind of beetle on its back, except he'd run back in time to intervene. Christ! A tinge of impatience in Bart's voice but at once fleeting, gone.

In the neurologist's suite, Louisa Hansen and her son Bart are a familiar pair. The receptionist greets them by name. The nurses greet them by name. "My son." Louisa clutches his arm tight at the elbow when the nurse calls her name, the tall looming darkly handsome young son, and she the ravage-faced mother, a Pietà in reverse. "My son will accompany me into Dr. Kraukauer's office."

THE FLATBED

For Henri Cole

She liked to envision him in this way.

Some sort of flatbed. Like the kind hooked behind a small truck.

And he's on the flatbed in some kind of arrangement of chains securing his wrists and ankles so he can't move.

He's sitting up, chained. An awkward posture that must strain his back, neck, legs.

His head is lifted, his eyes are alert and aware.

The flatbed is being hauled along the interstate.

Wet snow has begun to fall. No wind, the snow falls vertically out of a gunmetal sky, mostly melting on the ground.

Who is driving the truck, he can't see.

He's trapped there on the flatbed. Can't move except to jerk his shoulders and head and tug against the chains making his wrists and ankles bloody. He has screamed—but no longer. His throat is raw, he is exhausted.

Snow on his face like melting tears.

* * *

Would G. know where he was being hauled, on the flatbed?

Would G. guess it was to a slaughterhouse?

He said, Is it me? Must be.

He was N. who'd come into her life unexpectedly.

He was one in a sequence of men. Most she eluded and re-buffed and found reasons to dislike, or they suddenly disliked her—one of them said bitterly *A beautiful face doesn't give you the right.*

She hadn't had to ask *The right to what?*

Or suddenly she was afraid of them, of what is called *leading a man on.*

For no man likes to be *led on.*

But N. was different, she had no idea why. N., she found herself thinking of, often. Maybe it was an ordinary sort of female yearning. Maybe it was her fear of being left alone or discovered to be a dirty girl, that's to say a badly dirtied girl, past redemption. Or maybe (this was a thought she could hardly acknowledge) she was falling in love with N. as a young woman might fall in love with a man.

A normal young woman. In love with a man.

But now it had gone wrong. She was stricken with guilt, shame.

For again it happened. Again, her body resisted the man. It was a subtle stiffening of her body, the tension of one poised at the brink of a dangerous action: diving from a high board, for instance.

It was not an obvious rejection of the man, or a rebuff. It was subtle, yet unmistakable. Every molecule in her body shuddering *No no no.*

And she began to shiver. The shivering was convulsive, and unstoppable.

Her way of combating it—the convulsive, ridiculous shivering in her own bed, in the man's arms—was to clench her jaws tight. If relaxed, her jaws would tremble, her teeth would chatter.

What chagrin, her body shutting up as it did. Like the body of a frightened child.

And the chattering teeth, with another as a witness, so intimate. She said, No. It isn't you. I . . .

There was a pause. N. was listening to her intently. His breathing was hoarse, harried.

She could not bring herself to say *It isn't you, I love you.*

He said, Well. Then there is something you haven't told me. She said, I don't think so.

Amending then, for this sounded too defensive, I—I don't know. I don't think so but I don't really know.

Something you haven't revealed to me yet.

His hands on her, tentative, caressing. As you might lay hands on a frightened and shivering dog, to comfort; to contain, calm, and comfort; and in the strength of the hands, a certain confidence, assurance.

Somebody hurt you, I'm guessing. D'you want to tell me about it?

How many times, she hadn't wished to count.

There had been the mortifying first time, when she'd been nineteen years old—*old* for a first-time sexual experience. And there'd been a second time, and a third—and each time baffling, humiliating.

This was perhaps only the fourth time. But it seemed to her the final time. She was twenty-nine years old: she would have no more chances.

As a young girl she'd been diffident about sex. She'd been uncomfortable hearing other girls talk about sex, her friends had laughed at her.

As an older girl she'd become adept at avoiding sexual circumstances. She grew to like the company of boys and men, and they liked her company, usually—but it was not a good idea to pursue this attraction, she'd learned.

To mislead another is cruel. To entice, and to repel—this could be dangerous.

For she could not anticipate the reaction of her body. Even if she'd had a few drinks. Even if she felt *loving*.

The clenching of pelvic muscles involuntary as the blinking of an eye when the eye is touched. The panicked withdrawal, recoil.

As if the man touching her, seeking entry into her body, was an instrument of harm, torture—to be repelled.

The panic reflex. The convulsive shivering. She was helpless in thrall to a terrible suffocating fear as the sexual part of her, which had seemed so alive, so yearning, as if thrumming with desire for the man, had shut up like a fist.

No. It was her body's mute cry—*No.*

An aroused male would have the right to be seriously pissed. Seriously offended. He'd have the right to extricate himself from the female, throw on his God damned clothes and depart and not return.

She could not protest. She could barely murmur *Sorry.*

At the bottom of the pit she lay helpless. Her body was a child's body, in terror of violation. Clenched tight, shivering.

N. was saying, Will you tell me? Who has hurt you?

She told him no one. Please.

No one? I don't believe that.

She'd managed to control the shivering. Clenching her jaws tight so that her teeth couldn't chatter. *That* was an accomplishment, in these mortifying circumstances.

Until at last N. said, Hey: it's OK. We'll be fine.

N. spoke genially, with a kind of forced cheer. For this, she loved him.

Though he was somewhat mysterious to her—not a man she knew well, except intimately.

She'd calculated that he was at least fifteen years older than she was. She'd gathered that he was the father of children; divorced, and the children near-grown. Some bitterness—personal, legal—regarding the ex-wife. And there'd been a domestic trag-edy in his life—the death of a child.

To which he'd alluded but of which he had given her to know he did not care to speak, just yet.

Just now he'd seemed to understand, and to forgive. Her body's clenching against his touch was not a clenching against *him*.

The last man who'd touched her in this way, who had tried to make love to her, whom she hadn't liked so much as she liked N., had been sulky, sullen—rudely asking if she'd seen a doctor about this—*problem*.

Asking if it was a *problem* she'd had in the past?

What measures had she taken, or tried to take, to deal with the *problem*.

Sexual frigidity. Fear.

Sexual terror, phobia.

Can't breathe. Can't bear it.

Sorry sorry.

No man wanted to think that it was he whom the woman's body was rejecting. It was necessary to think that the woman had a *problem*—physical, mental.

Yet N. was saying, We just need to go slow, I think. Slower.

Through a buzzing in her ears like cicadas she heard herself murmur *yes*.

I'm a big man. I'm heavy. Heavier than I look. Maybe I scare you. Maybe your body thinks it's being crushed. We can figure some other way. When, you know—you think you're ready.

Heard herself murmur weakly *yes*.

We have plenty of time, right? There's no urgency about any of this.

No urgency! She wanted to think so.

Except: *I am twenty-nine years old not nine years old. I want my life to begin.*

She and N. had known each other for approximately eighteen months. Not as lovers nor even as friends but as acquaintances brought into contact through a professional association in which she, the younger, the female, was a new employee and he, the elder, the male, had a position of authority.

Not that N. was her boss. N. was her superior of course but the chain of command didn't link N. and her directly.

The intersection between non-profit and private. *He* was the private.

Was it true there was no urgency between them? There is always an urgency to sexual love.

He would find another, she thought. There were so many women.

Young, unattached. In the early stages of their careers.

And there were other women, single, divorced, even widowed —a man like N. would not have to look far.

Yet, N. had seemed to be attracted to her immediately. A shrewd hunter-look had come into his eyes when he'd first approached her at a reception She'd come alone, in black: black silk skirt falling to nearly her ankles, sleeveless black silk top and over it a black velvet jacket that fit her narrow torso like a glove. Her ash-colored hair she'd braided and twisted around her head. He'd greeted her, and peered at her quizzically—he hadn't recognized her at first as one of the young women of the arts foundation, too junior to have a title other than assistant. Then, he'd seemed embarrassed. He said, I'm sorry—I thought you were someone else.

Wittily she'd said, Yes? Who?

Between them something seemed to have been decided. Though they'd spoken to others at the reception they met again as others were leaving and N. said, Have dinner with me? Hey?

She wanted to think that N. was right: there was no urgency between them.

But when they tried to make love another time and her body recoiled—what then?

She was deeply ashamed of her sexual shyness. If that was what it was.

She had never gone to a therapist. The very thought was repugnant to her, such *weakness*.

It was wonderful to her, that N. seemed to forgive her. Kissing her and caressing her, comforting her and trying to warm her so that she stopped shivering. Wonderful, this man was on her side.

She'd heard N. had a quick temper. She had not yet witnessed it but she'd heard from others at the arts foundation, who'd been astonished and impressed at the way N. was capable of speaking at meetings, cutting off slow-speaking individuals, interrupting or contradicting others. One of his favored words was *Bullshit*. Another was *Fine!*—meaning the discussion was ended.

It was said of N. that he never attacked younger employees but only individuals of his own approximate rank.

It was said *You wouldn't want to cross him.*

In N.'s arms she lay shivering, less convulsively now. The panic fit was passing.

The bedclothes that had been freshly laundered when she'd made the bed earlier that day were now humid, sticky. A ceiling fan turned wanly overhead. It was an unusually warm autumn. Their bodies were naked and hopeful—or had been. Now they clutched at each other like exhausted swimmers washed to shore.

She felt the fatty flesh at N's waist, and at his back: sinewy little knobs of flesh, and bumps and indentations across his back. Sparse coarse hairs scattered on his back, in striations across his sides. How strange, to be caressing the naked body of a man whom she scarcely knew, yet imagined she might love!

All love is desperation. This is our secret.

Her fingers groped for his penis, that had been so hard a minute before; now limp, soft-skinned, and vulnerable; and his fingers closed over hers in what she felt to be a kind of rebuke, gently pushing away.

Saying, Maybe we need a drink. Maybe that would help.

She wasn't sure that she had anything to drink in the loft. A friend had brought a bottle of red wine to celebrate her moving into these new quarters in a refurbished warehouse overlooking the river but that had been months ago, she'd never opened the bottle and wasn't even sure where it was.

Drinking was not a solace for her. Or, drinking would be too wonderful a solace, she had better not begin.

He had urged her to drink. A little sip of his drink. On their walks, a stop at a *taverna,* as he called it, or a *bistro,* and how delightful, the little girl sipping from the older gentleman's wineglass, until she began to cough, choke.

Then, he'd given her chocolate mints. To disguise the smell of the wine.

Our secret. Just the little darling and me.

N. said, Tell me what you're thinking, Ceille. Just now.

She couldn't recall. What had she been thinking?

She said, I love the sound of my name when you say it. For the first time, I love my name.

Neither made a move to detach from the other. N. would fall asleep kissing her.

That the man so trusted her, felt comfortable with her, after even this clumsy episode, was deeply moving to her.

Badly she wanted to sleep, in the man's arms. It was very late: nearing 2 A.M. But she was not so comfortable. Her skin chafed against his. His thick-sounding breathing would keep her awake though she was relieved to hear it close beside her as if this were N.'s bed in N.'s life and she had been taken in by N.

Her brain was alive with thoughts, brittle darting thoughts like nails that flew about to no purpose. Often in intimate situations this was the case, with another person.

Fear of the other. His strength, and the surprise of what he will ask from you.

What he will execute upon you, without asking.

And still she was cold. Her fingers and toes like ice.

Huddled against the man's warm body, a solid sizable body, taking up more than half of her bed.

So cold! Bone-marrow cold!

As if her life, a still-young life, were veering to a premature ending like a runaway vehicle on a twisting mountain road where you can see only a few yards ahead for the way is blind and the descent from the road steep and irrevocable.

Wanting to plead with this deep-slumbering man in her bed *Love me anyway—can't you? I think—I can love you.*

She'd never told anyone. Not ever.

She'd known better. Already by the age of—had it been seven? eight? ten?—that it would be a mistake to *tell.*

For once you *tell*, you can't take back what you have *told.*

In the household, in the family. And it was a large family.

A family so large, if you shut your eyes and tried to assemble them all in the living room, standing and seated in a half-circle around the ceiling-high Christmas tree, you could not.

For always there are shadowy figures, vague and undefined at the periphery of the scene. Always, tall male figures whose faces are just slightly blurred.

You could identify them perhaps. But you could not truly see them.

Sometimes these figures are sitting. In fact, sitting on the floor.

In some juxtaposition to the glittering Christmas tree. The astonishment of the Christmas tree, that so glittered and gleamed and the fragrance of its still-living needles so powerful, just recalling makes you want to cry.

Eyes filled with moisture. The trip of a heartbeat.

Want to cry but will not cry. Not ever *cry*.

For she was a shy child. Shy, and shrewd. You might mistake shyness for slowness, reticence for stupidity, physical wariness for physical ineptitude, but you'd have been mistaken.

He had counseled her *This is our secret. These are good times but secret.*

He had warned her *This is our secret. These are good times but secret.*

And so she had not ever told.

(For who was there to tell? Not her nervous mother, not her irritable father. Often they smiled startled seeing her before them as if she were a surprise to them, a happy surprise, amid so many other surprises that were not happy; as if somehow they'd forgotten her, and the sight of her was a happy reminder; for she'd been led to believe from a young age that she was the one happy thing in their lives, despite being an "accident" in their lives—*I think we were burnt-out, almost—with the marriage— playing house—we'd had our kids, we thought: four of them! Jesus! And then—our darling . . .*)

(And later, in grade school, when still it was happening to her, still she was in thrall to him-whose-identity-she-could-not-reveal, she could not have told her teachers, nor could she have told another child, even her best friends—especially not her best friends. From the experiences of others who'd had far less significant secrets to reveal she'd learned how *telling* flew back in the face of the *teller* like spitting in the wind. Forever afterward you were the one who'd *told,* the *tattletale;* and what had been done to you would be irrevocably mixed up in the minds of others with *you.*)

No one knew. No one wished to know. No one asked *her.*

The family was large, and well-to-do. The name *Bankcroft* was attached to a downtown street and a square and a dignified old office building. *Bankcroft* exuded an air of satisfaction, pride.

Brothers, sisters, cousins, aunts and uncles, and grandparents.

These were highly sociable people. Most evenings there were visitors in the big old Victorian house.

In such circumstances you would think that a little girl so frequently singled out for special attention by a (male, older) relative would be observed. But you would be mistaken.

Our baby. Our darling. I'm shamelessly spoiling her—she's my last baby.

Everyone adores her! They just can't help it.

Her mother certainly adored her. But mostly when others were present. At the start of dinner parties she was shown off—her curly ash-blond hair, her special party dress and fancy little shoes—then carried away upstairs by a nanny hired for such purposes.

To have *told* her mother! She could not.

For she could foresee: the look in her mother's face.

Surprise, hurt, disbelief. *No no no no no*—this could never be.

To have *told* her father! Absolutely *no*.

All this she would have to explain to N. If she did not, she would lose him.

And if she did, very likely she would lose him just the same.

Yes of course, as a child she'd been taken to a doctor periodically.

A (male) family doctor, pediatrician. An acquaintance of her mother's and so, during the visits, in the examination room, her mother and Dr. T. chatted.

The examinations were routine, perfunctory, non-traumatic. The examinations did not involve an inspection of the child's body inside her clothing for why would one do such a thing? With the child's mother present, friendly and sociable?

Visits to Dr. T's office usually involved a "booster" vaccine, possibly ear-wax removal.

She who was her mother's *darling* endured these visits to the doctor stoically. Young she'd learned the strategy of being mature beyond her years.

Later, as a young adolescent, she'd had to endure the ignominy and pain of a gynecological examination.

Here, the doctor was her mother's (female) doctor: obstetrician, gynecologist.

The examination of her small hard breasts had been both painful and humiliating but she'd managed to bear it without resistance only just biting hard on her lower lip to draw a little blood.

The pelvic exam had been so brutal, such a shock to her rigid-quivering body, in horror and disbelief she'd begun to cry, laugh, hyperventilate—this could not possibly be happening to her, that which was happening to her—*worse, far worse, more painful and more terrifying than what had been perpetrated on her as a child, which she'd begun to forget;* the examination had had to be terminated for the delicate-boned girl was squirming, thrashing, kicking in hysterics, in danger of injuring both the examining doctor and herself.

Her mother had accompanied her to the gynecologist's office but now that she was fourteen, and so seemingly self-composed, she'd asked her mother to please remain out in the waiting room. Now her poor shocked mother had to be hurriedly summoned into the examination room by one of the nurses.

It took some minutes to calm the hysterical girl. Her blood pressure had been taken at the start of the examination and had been one hundred over sixty; after the bout of hysterics her blood pressure was one hundred thirty-six over sixty.

The doctor who was her mother's friend was both concerned and annoyed.

Telling her mother to take her home. The examination was over.

She's had a shock. She's extremely sensitive. Maybe some other time I can do a pelvic exam. But not today.

She'd had to comfort her mother on the way home. Assuring her mother that she would have no "traumatic" memories of the assault.

And afterward she'd overheard, by chance, her mother telling her father, in a rueful tone *At least we know she's a virgin!*

Yet, years later, when she was living alone and went alone to a (female) gynecologist for a routine examination, virtually the same thing happened: shock, hysterics.

Except then, for God's sake, she'd been twenty-three years old.

Though technically still a virgin but no longer a skittish young teenager.

Usually, she avoided doctors. She was in "perfect health"—so she believed. But for medical insurance purposes, in connection with her new employment, she'd had to have a routine physical examination and this included a gynecological examination.

Again, she'd managed to endure the breast exam. But the pelvic exam was as brutal as she'd recalled. The gynecologist was a young Chinese-American woman, very skilled, soft-spoken; she'd explained what she was doing, as if to mollify her tense patient; she'd shown her the speculum—(was that the word? the very sound of it made her tremble)—that was an instrument of torture to her, a crude caricature of the male penis, unbearable. Involuntarily, on the examination table, feet in stirrups and knees raised and parted, she'd recoiled as she had at the age of fourteen; her lower lip would ooze blood afterward, where she'd almost bitten through it.

The young-woman gynecologist had been concerned. She couldn't complete the examination, she hadn't been able to get a Pap swab, there was no way to know if the young woman shivering and shuddering on the examination table had a vaginal infection, or—something more serious.

I'm so sorry! My God. Please forgive me. We can try again.

It was the voice of reason. Her best self. But the child-self, quivering with hurt, in dread of further hurt, was always there, waiting for the collapse of the best, adult self.

But she'd managed. She had gripped the edges of the leather examination table and held her trembling knees parted as the gynecologist re-inserted the speculum, to open her vagina, to open it terribly as a delicate flower might be opened, exposed to a harsh killing sun.

What relief then, the speculum was withdrawn!

Am I bleeding? But bleeding doesn't last.

It's normal to bleed and the blood to coagulate.

Yet, there was more to the exam. The gynecologist had not yet finished. Inserting her rubber fingers into the young woman's vagina, pressing against her lower abdomen to determine if there were tumorous growths, irregularities. And, at the end, a rectal exam—swiftly executed and less painful.

In the vagina were scars, fine as hairs, faded scars—and in the soft moist walls of the uterus. So the gynecologist said, puzzled.

Have you had an illness, an infection? This would have been some years ago, perhaps.

Shook her head *no*. Did not know.

Or some sort of—accident? Or . . .

There was a long pause. An awkward pause.

Until Dr. Chen said, It's healed now. Whatever it was, it has healed. Do you have pain with sexual intercourse?

Shook her head *no*. Frowning and vague as if to suggest *That is a private matter, doctor!*

The gynecologist regarded her with an expression of—was it sympathy? Pity?

She thought *This woman knows. She is my sister.*

Carefully Dr. Chen said, Do you have any questions to ask me? We will receive the results of the Pap test in a few days and we will call you.

The dreaded exam was over. In triumph the shaken young woman sat up on the leather table, tissue-paper bristling beneath her buttocks. A smear of lubricant, a barely visible smear of blood on the paper.

Thank you, doctor.

She'd gone away smiling. Whistling.

These good times no one will know. Our secret.

The Pap test came back negative. It was a confirmed fact, she was in perfect health.

No need to see any doctor for a long, long time.

N. said, We have to talk.

Gravely and profoundly N. fixed his gaze upon her. He'd urged her to sit down, to be still. For there was a need for her, in N.'s presence, to be always moving about, to a window, for instance, to glance nervously down into the street. The sound of a phone ringing, in a neighboring loft, was distracting to her.

Wanting to tell him, to amuse him, that she'd had a "stalker" once—when she'd still been a university student.

Foreign-born, dusky-skinned, lonely-looking. He'd waited for her in stairwells, on the sidewalk in front of the residence hall. (He'd been a graduate or post-doc, she thought, in something unimaginably difficult—molecular biology, computational neuroscience.) She'd smiled at him in her careless way and he'd followed her home and thereafter for much of her senior year he'd hung about with yearning doggy-eyes and her roommates had been concerned for her *Aren't you worried? Shouldn't we report him to security?* And she'd laughed saying *Don't be silly. He'll give up soon.*

Through a rustling in her brain N. was saying gravely, Look, I love you. We have to talk.

Love you had the air of a mild rebuke. He was chiding her, as you would a small stubborn self-destructive child.

Frowning, N. said, You aren't being honest with me. If you care for me, as I care for you, we have to be honest with each other.

Care for me. Care for you. These words were giddy in her ears, she was stricken to the heart.

She'd never *told*. She could not begin now, at her ridiculous age.

He had never threatened to hurt her, exactly. The tall (male) figure of her childhood. She was sure he'd never hurt or injured her, it was bizarre to suggest that he'd inserted something into her tiny child's vagina so sharp that it had left miniature scars; her mother, or one of her older sisters, would have discovered bloodstains on her panties and all would have been exposed.

Though this individual, this tall (male) figure so predominant in the life of her family, alone of his (older) generation insisting upon sitting on the floor, Indian-style on the thick carpet in front of the Christmas tree, with the kids. An individual whom her mother greatly respected, adored, and to a degree feared; a man whom her father greatly admired, though G. had never been particularly friendly to him.

Which was a mystery, since G. was her father's father.

Good times our secret. Ours.

And so, she'd never told. In recent years when she tried to recall what *it* was—exactly what had been done to her, and with her; what sorts of things he'd shown her, and spoken of to her—she'd discovered that she remembered very little at all.

There was such banality to it—"recovered" memory.

Or was it "repressed" memory.

She'd never tried to explain to any man. Never to any of the boys with whom she'd been friendly in high school. Boys who'd been attracted to her in ways flattering to her even as she understood *They don't know me. How disgusted they would be, if they knew me.*

But she could not. She could not *tell.* Not only was she repelled by the prospect of *telling,* she would have faltered and fumbled for words. For, when she'd been a little girl, and entrusted to this tall dignified relative, a kind of blindness had come over her, amnesia like a fine pale mist—she could not really remember clearly what he'd done to her only the air of furtive excitement, anxiety, and elation. *That he was getting away with it. Under the noses of the family. His family! That was part of the attraction.*

All that she could remember of those years was both faded and over-bright, like a photograph of an exploding nova. You understood that there was something inside the blinding light but you could not see it. You could not identify it.

He'd given her gifts. Countless gifts. He'd taken her to *The Nutcracker* each year at the War Memorial. And to *A Christmas Carol*.

He'd taken her sisters and her brother to some of these occasions, as well. He'd given them presents. He'd pressed his forefinger against his lips, smiling *Don't be jealous, darling! It's to make them think that they are your equal though we know better.*

He'd been clever. He'd never been suspected—not once.

She'd been made to know that she was special. That was the secret.

And now she did not want to acknowledge herself as a victim. In this era of victims, "survivors." She could not identify herself as one of them. She was too accomplished a young woman, and too promising—in her career, in which she had an excellent job helping to oversee the funding of arts projects, if not in her private life. If she'd been visibly wounded, crippled—she would have stubbornly denied it. For she did not want pity, or sympathy.

She would explain to N. that she could not tell him who he'd been, the man who had despoiled her life. She could not share with him such memories.

And of course, she wasn't certain. She remembered—some things. But in patches, like broken clouds.

Broken clouds blown swiftly across the sky. You crane your neck to observe as the clouds are blown away and disappear.

Oddly she did recall G.'s voice, sometimes. In others' voices, she heard G.'s voice. His grunted words. And pleas—she remembered pleas. (But these were not his. These were hers.) In the speeches of politicians she heard the thrilling timbre of his voice, the voice of a public man, even when he'd retired from public office.

The fact was, G. had been a locally renowned man. *Bankcroft* the revered name.

All of the family was proud of that name. She, too, had been proud of that name except in secret she'd been ashamed of that name for it was *his* name, as it was her own.

She would not tell N.: a ten-year-old child is capable of considering suicide.

Killing oneself isn't such a secret now. Not such a taboo. A child is well aware of suicide attempts, and of successful suicides. As a child is aware of death generally. And betrayal.

She'd moved 360 miles away from *Bankcroft Street, Bankcroft Square,* the *Bankcroft Building.*

Yes, she'd been proud that G. had so favored *her*. You would have been proud, too.

They'd sung together, on their walks. G. had taught her "You Are My Sunshine," "White Christmas," "Tea for Two." Jaunty tunes were G.'s specialty. Hand in hand. She had not ever tried to run away. She had not ever tried to wrest her hand from his, and run away.

Through the cemetery she might have run. Run run run until her little heart burst and she fell amid the weatherworn old grave markers striking her head, cracking her skull so the bad memories leaked out like black blood.

He had not ever injured her. His finger inserted inside her to tickle, that was all.

Tickle tickle! That's my good little girl.

Of all that G. had told her, the stream of words, chatter and banter, teasing and cajoling, years later she would recall virtually nothing.

The grunts, she did remember.

And when they'd been alone together—(when he'd managed to arrange that they were alone together: could be a visit to Cross Memorial Cemetery to the grave of his dear departed wife who'd been buried beneath a shiny salmon-colored grave marker)—he hadn't felt the need for words.

His hand gripping hers had been sufficient. No need for words.

Plunged to a place beyond language where even his careful cautious demeanor dissolved, spittle gathered in the corners of his mouth, and his eyes rolled white beyond the dignified gold-rimmed glasses.

N. said, You're thinking of him now. You're remembering.

She denied this. Guiltily, weakly she denied this.

No. You're thinking of him now. Tell me who he is!

N. was becoming impatient, angry. She had not guessed at the start of their relationship how aggressive N. might be, how possessive of her.

197

She would have risen, walked quickly away. But N. seized her hands in his and held her in place.

Tell me who he was. What happened.

Her hands, gripped by his. She felt a swirl of vertigo.

Whoever it was—the bastard! Tell me.

She was not adept at lying. Bold frank outright lies. She was no good at such. But she'd become adept at another sort of lie, shrewdly nuanced, ambiguous. The lie that is an omission, a failure to totally recall.

Yet even this she could not risk. For N. seemed to see into her innermost heart.

Someone hurt you. Sexually. Or—in some other way, as well as sexual. Tell me.

I did tell you! I told you *no*.

Something that went wrong, something that left a wound. Not a scar that has healed. A bleeding wound.

I am not a—bleeding wound. Don't do this to me.

N. was smiling at her. But N. was not smiling with her.

He was older than she was: yet not old, only just in his early forties. A still-young, vigorous man. A man whose physical being seemed trapped, or in any case contained and repressed, inside his proper businessman clothing: expensive suits, shoes.

His background had been, he'd said, working-class.

Or maybe just a little lower.

Immigrant grandparents, and his father had worked with his hands most of his life and had wanted to be, for a few years in adolescence, a professional boxer.

He, N., had tried boxing at a neighborhood gym. In high school.

He'd loved it. Hitting, and even, to a degree, getting hit. But there were guys in the neighborhood, black kids, some of them built like Mike Tyson at age fifteen-sixteen—they'd discouraged N., you might say.

So, he'd quit. Probably just in time, before he'd gotten seriously hurt.

His hair was thick, sleekly brushed back across his furrowed scalp. She could see the boxer-hunter in him now: the way his eyes were fixed upon her.

She was frightened of him, in that instant.

She'd thought him husbandly, fatherly. But there was something else now, a deeper and more primitive being.

She said, I—I can't remember. . . .

What? What can't you remember?

. . . what happened, or . . .

When? When was this, that you can't remember?

Not recently. Not for a long time.

And who was it?

Who was it?—no one . . .

Fuck that! Tell me.

Oh he's an old man now—he isn't the man who. . . .

She was laughing. Her face was bright as a flame, her very hair seemed to stir on her head, like upright flames. He was staring at her in triumph, he had won. He had overpowered her, he had obliterated her opposition to him. Never in her life had she uttered such things—it was unbelievable to her, she'd said so much. Secrets snatched from her, irremediably. Her burning face she hid, she wiped at her eyes. Bright laughter fell from her mouth like broken glass.

She'd twisted her hands out of his grip, but now she seized his hands, his large hot hands, and held them tight.

In a lowered voice she said, I never told anyone.

He said, Until now.

He deserves to die. Anyone who harms a child.
  But you promised!
  Fuck my promise. That was before.

And then he was saying, I promise not to harm him. But I would like to talk to him.

She called home. A rarity in recent years.

She preferred e-mail. Though she did not often write to her parents, either.

At once her mother heard something in her voice. Her mother asked what was wrong, why was she calling so late in the evening, was it an emergency?—sounding both frightened and annoyed.

A mother's first thought is *Pregnant*!

She said, No! It is not an emergency.

She said, The emergency was years ago. Not now.

Her mother said, Emergency? What are you talking about, Cecie?

Tell me how G. is. I don't hear about G. much any longer.

G. was Grandfather. Or, as he'd liked to be called, with a French flourish, *Grandpapa*.

He's—well. I mean, reasonably well, for his age. He's just returned from—I think it was the Amalfi Coast. He'd gone on a tour, with friends. He's still involved in politics, behind the scenes. You know how the Brankrofts are! He comes to dinner here at least twice a week and sometimes after mass we have brunch at the High Bridge Inn. I wish he and your father got along better together but he just—sort of—ignores Matt. He asks after you . . .

Does he? Does he ask after me?

Of course. Grandpapa always asks after you.

What does he ask?

What does he *ask*? Just how are you doing, your work, are you engaged, or seeing someone—the usual questions.

He wants to know if I'm "engaged" or "seeing someone"? And why is that his business?

Your grandfather asks after all his grandchildren, now that so many of you are scattered and living far away.

But me, he asks after *me*?

Why are you asking me this, Cecie? Why now?

I think you must know why.

What do you mean? I—I don't know why. . . .

Why didn't he ever remarry, after Grandma died? Wasn't anyone good enough for him? All those rich widows!

Why are you asking such questions? Why about your grandfather? You sound so angry, Cecie. . . .

No. I'm not angry. Why would I be angry?

I have no idea, Cecie. You've always had this way about you—this unpredictable short temper—first you call late, you must know a phone ringing past eleven P.M. usually means bad news, and now—

She interrupted saying, I think I'll hang up now.

Please, wait—

I'm sorry to disturb you, Mother. You're right, it's late. Good night!

None of them knows. None will guess.
Our secret is safe little darling sealed with a kiss.

She told N.: It isn't an issue in my life. I never think of it, truly.

Bullshit. You think of it all the time.

N. touched her. His warm broad hand across her belly, a lover's casual caress and she stiffened at once.

All the time you are thinking of it. I could see it in your face, before I spoke to you.

She wanted to protest: she was always so much more than whatever had been perpetrated upon her.

A fact she kept to herself, to nourish herself like something warm—a heated stone, or medallion—a kind of shield—pressed against her breasts and belly, secreted beneath her clothing.

She took pride in all that she was, that had nothing to do with the naively trusting little girl she'd been more than fifteen years ago.

For instance, she was a swimmer: almost a serious swimmer. In the dark of winter she rose early to swim in the university pool, for which she paid a yearly fee since she'd graduated from the university with a master's degree in social psychology.

In the shimmering water, her body dissolved into pure sensation, the strength of her muscled arms and legs to keep her afloat and to propel her forward. Once, N. would observe her swimming in the university pool, in the early morning, and would stare in surprised admiration. For her body was sleek, slender, and yet strong—this was not the body of a female victim. *If you've been thinking you know me, you are mistaken.*

And she took pride in her professional career. Such as it was.

(And was G., too, proud of her? She had to suppose so. Her mother continued to forward greetings from G. to her; occasional cards, presents. He'd learned her latest address in order to send her a lavish bouquet of two dozen yellow roses in celebration of her appointment at the arts foundation. She'd shocked friends by gaily tossing into the trash.)

She had her job. Her new position. She loved books— nineteenth-century novels, classics—her favorites were *Bleak House, Middlemarch, Tess of the D'Urbervilles,* and *Jude the Obscure.* She could reread these, late at night when she couldn't sleep; or she could watch the late-night Classic Film channel—Cary

Grant, Greer Garson, Spencer Tracy, Katharine Hepburn, Humphrey Bogart, Clark Gable, Rita Hayworth. Their faces were comforting to her, like the faces of distant relatives.

Several times she'd seen *The Red Shoes*. Mesmerized and deeply moved.

She felt a perverse sympathy for the murderous lovers of *Double Indemnity*. Each time she saw the film the ending came to her as a shock—for it might so easily have been another kind of ending.

She went to gallery openings. She went to poetry readings. She bought books for the poets to sign, which she kept in a special place in her loft apartment, on a window sill in the sun.

What are these? N. asked curiously.

She selected one of the slender books, opened it as if casually, and read lines of surpassing beauty and wonder:

> What a fine performance they gave!
> Though they didn't know where they were going,
>   they made their prettiest song of all.

N. asked what did this mean? Was it a happy poem?
She said, I think so. Yes.

Another thing about her, another special thing, to set her off from the pack of other good-looking young women, Cielle dressed exclusively in black.

*   *   *

She told him about the flatbed. A man chained on the flatbed behind a truck hauled on the interstate.

He whistled between his teeth. Where's the man being taken, to a slaughterhouse?

Yes. To a slaughterhouse.

But do you get that far? In the dream, I mean.

No. It's just the flatbed behind the truck, and him on it chained and knowing where he's being taken. He has plenty of time to think about where's he's being taken and what will be done to him then.

But you've never gotten that far.

He seemed to be goading her into saying *Not yet*.

They were lying together on her bed. On the rainbow afghan on her bed. There were ways of intimacy, ways of avoiding her sexual fear, they were learning, in compensation.

In each other's arms not fully undressed. As a parent might comfort a fretting child so N. comforted her. Kissing her forehead, the hot pit of her neck that made her laugh wildly, and squirm.

It wasn't your fault, Ceille. I hope you know that.

She knew. She wished to think so.

A young child, an adult—there is no way that a child can "consent." The law recognizes this. And the moral law.

She smiled. She laughed. For G. had quoted a German philosopher to her once, in one of his playful extravagant moods in which he pretended that she wasn't a little girl but an adult and an equal—"*The starry heavens above me, and the moral law within me.*"

Why G. had quoted Immanuel Kant to her, she had no idea.

Only just he was a highly successful public man who tired of being public and accountable and responsible and adult and so at these secret times he was playful and extravagant and could not be predicted in his behavior as he could not be reined in, or controlled.

He smelled of a sweet cologne dabbed on his clean-shaven jaws. You wanted to smile at this fragrance, or you wanted to hide your face and cry. His *tickle finger* was a special finger and the nail always kept clean and filed by G. himself with an emery board carried in his pocket.

You're thinking of him now, Ceille? Tell me.

She bit her lip. She would not.

It makes me sick, Ceille. When you think of him. When you're with me, like this, and God damn, you think of *him*.

She wanted to console him *Yes. It makes me sick, too.*

His name? Who he was, to you?

He was—he—

Her heart beat painfully. She was frightened she would faint.

—he was very clever. No one ever knew, or suspected. In all those years—six years. He was *trusted*.

And did he victimize other girls? What about your sisters?

No.

No? Are you sure?

She tried to think. She was laughing, this conversation was so ridiculous, years too late to matter.

Oh no. I mean—yes. I'm sure.

He hadn't adored them. They were older, less attractive.
I was his little darling!

It would not be unpremeditated. Therefore, it would have to be skillfully executed.

N. had a law degree. He'd practiced law for several years. He told her to contact the relative who'd molested her for six years and to arrange to meet him in a neutral place.

Quickly she said *no*.

Unless she said *The cemetery.*

N. asked if it was a cemetery where people would be likely to be visiting, where they might be observed.

She said no. Her grandmother had been buried in a part of the cemetery owned by the Bankcroft family and this was at the edge of the cemetery near a pine forest.

You won't hurt him? You will just speak with him.

That's right. Just speak with him.

G. must have thought it was strange, at last she called him. It had been years since they'd seen each other for of course she had avoided family gatherings as soon as she'd left home.

Cecelia! Is it you?

The shock in his voice. Yet the old warmth beneath, she'd forgotten.

She'd been very clever. She'd learned G.'s current telephone number in a circuitous way so that the fact that she'd sought out the number might not be immediately evident. She had not asked her mother or her father, for instance.

She heard herself say, I miss my old life, Grandpapa. I am having some hard times now. I am very lonely, Grandpapa.

Grandpapa. This had been the magic name.

Pronounced as if French. Emphasis upon *grand.*

Blithe and bright she spoke to the astonished man at the other end of the line. Asking to see him, so that she might introduce him to her fiancé who was a secret from the family.

Secret? But why?

When you meet him, you will know. I will trust in your intuition.

This was flattering to him, she knew. This was the silver hook in his fat wet lip, that would doom him.

In Cross Cemetery. We can meet there.

In Cross Cemetery?

Yes. Please.

But—why don't you come to the house first. . . .

At Grandma's grave, we can meet. Where we used to walk, Grandpapa, remember?

Of course I remember, darling. How could I forget?

Truly the old man was flattered, hypnotized. This slow hour of his old-man life and the phone had rung and it was his *little darling* calling him who had never in her life called him before.

I've kept up on your news, darling. Your mother keeps me informed. I know you've moved. I know you have a new job that sounds important but I would guess it probably doesn't pay much so if you need some money, darling—just let me know.

That would be very kind, Grandpapa. We could talk about that.

Before hanging up the phone she said suddenly, Oh I miss you, Grandpapa! So much.

Each would be away for the weekend. N. in New York City, Ceille in Washington, D.C.

So they told friends. So N. told his near-grown children.

In N.'s SUV they then drove west to Rochester. It was a clear, sunny, vivid autumn morning in October.

She'd had a sleepless night. She warmed her hands at the dashboard heating vent as N. drove.

She was distracted by a pickup truck speeding ahead of them. The flatbed of the truck, piled with what appeared to be lumber.

And the lumber secured to the flatbed by chains.

She said, as if she'd only just thought of this, He's older now. He isn't a danger now. I'm sure.

(She was not sure. She was certainly not sure of this.)

I've heard he has had medical problems. I think cancer of some kind—prostate, probably.

(Of this she was more certain. Her mother had kept her advised of her Grandpapa Bankcroft knowing how much he meant to her, far more than he meant to his other grandchildren.)

N. said, Of course he victimized other children. Before you, and after you.

N. said, You didn't tell. He'd terrified you, and you didn't tell. And so, another little girl was victimized after you. That is the pattern.

N. was not accusing her. Carefully he spoke, sympathetic.

Now we're breaking the pattern. This will end it.

She wasn't hearing this. She was thinking maybe it had been a mistake to have confessed to N. For now the secret had been revealed. She'd unfurled a precious garment to be trampled in the mud.

She laughed, shivering. She was very excited!

Playfully she warmed her icy fingers between his legs.

N. pushed her hands away. Don't distract me, darling. I'm trying to drive.

He'd made a reservation in a high-rise upscale hotel outside the city, eleventh floor overlooking the interstate and, in the distance, the serrated skyline of the city of Rochester. They were registered under a fictitious name as *Mr. & Mrs.*

Her love for N. was no longer a separate thing she could detach from her and hold at arm's length to contemplate.

Her love for N. had burrowed deep inside her. Her love for N. was inextricable from her fear of N.

In Cross Memorial Cemetery they saw him: the lone tall figure, still erect, well dressed, with a head of thick white hair. In his right hand he gripped an ebony cane in a way to suggest that the cane was mostly for show, not really needed.

He is only seventy-two or seventy-three, she said. He is not *old*.

Grandpapa had brought a pot of golden mums to the grave. The grandmother's grave.

It was famously known, locally—how grief-stricken G. had been, how heartbroken at the end of the long good marriage of forty-six years.

So good then, G. had had his family to console him. His young relatives, grandchildren.

On the graveled path they approached G. It was afternoon, the sky was amassing with clouds blown down from Lake Ontario. The last visitors were leaving the cemetery.

Now G. had sighted them. G. was alert and staring at them. At her. Slow happy recognition came into his face like candlelight.

Hi, Grandpapa!

Cecilia!

He moved to her, just perceptibly favoring his right leg. He would have taken her hand extended to him to squeeze her hand in greeting—but N. stepped between them.

Don't touch her!

White-haired G. stiffened. His smile faded.

His face was fine-creased, clean-shaven. He was a handsome old man who did not look his age. She felt a touch of vertigo in his presence.

N. was addressing G. calmly. Yet you could feel the mounting anger.

N.'s anger was inward, secret. Like N.'s love, that was indistinguishable from possession.

G. began to stammer to N. Foolish words were shaped by the old-man lips and wattles in the old-man face trembled.

She stood a little behind N. She saw that her grandfather had forgotten her in the exigency of the moment.

I—I have no idea what you are talking about, sir. Keep your voice down, please.

G. was indignant but G. was pleading. She was remembering how she and her family had heard G.'s voice frequently on the local radio news; they'd seen him often on television. He'd been a politician—township council, U.S. congressman on the Republican ticket—in the prime of his career.

G. was backing away from N. now. G. was visibly shaken—this was not the reception he'd anticipated.

His favorite granddaughter and her fiancé!—her secret fiancé. Introduced to *him*.

Wanting a blessing from *him*.

With a shaky hand G. was tugging a handkerchief out of a pocket, dabbing at his nose.

A red-veined nose, this was. Still handsome and still youthful but broken capillaries marred the clean-shaven skin and the alert eyes were ringed in creases.

He said, I have no idea what you are talking about, sir. If you don't desist, I will call 911.

N. spoke further. N. was accusing G. of certain acts—"repeated statutory rape"—"sexual assault upon a minor."

G. said indignantly, What has the girl been telling you! I did nothing to be ashamed of.

He said, Those were lost years. The girl was lonely.

Turning away with a look of wounded dignity. And the fear beneath.

Turning away on the graveled path clutching at his cane hoping that the confrontation had ended, he would be allowed to leave; that N., the girl's fiancé, advancing upon him, was going to let him go.

I want him to shit his pants. To be that scared.

The savagery of these words shocked her. She had no idea where they had come from.

She was hanging back, very excited. The shivering had begun, her teeth were chattering. She saw the chagrin, sick-guilt, yet righteousness in her grandfather's face. No! They could not let him walk away.

He would have walked away except N. sprang after him. The joy in N.'s face as he grabbed the fancy shining-ebony cane.

Sir! What are you—

Fuck you, old man! You're not going anywhere.

Foolishly G. tried to retrieve the cane. N. swung the cane at him, striking his head, his shoulders. Swift and deadly and unerring and paying no heed to the old man's pleas.

She was hiding her face. A little girl peeking through her fingers.

In the parking lot the last of the cemetery visitors were driving away. This was a good-luck sign: a blessing.

She was telling N. it was enough, now.

N. paid not the slightest heed to her. He did not hear her at all.

With a kind of sick fascination she held back. She saw her lover N. striking G., who'd been *Grandpapa*. She wanted to cry *No! Stop! He did love me.*

Within seconds the white-haired man had fallen. Still N. continued to strike at him, cursing.

The white-haired man on hands and knees in the grass. Desperately trying to crawl, to escape amid the gravestones.

N. stooped over him, now striking him with his closed fist. You filthy son of a bitch. You disgusting old pervert. Inflicting yourself on a little girl—you bastard! She shut her eyes, she could not bear to see the white-haired man so humiliated, broken.

Yet there was pleasure in this: so swiftly happening after the stasis of years.

And still G. was pleading. Not to her but to N., whom he had never seen before in his life and whose taut furious face would be the last face he saw.

She should have intervened. Beforehand, she knew she would feel this way, afterward.

Yet she did not move. Eagerly her eyes were fixed on the fallen man, the bright exploding blood from his scalp, his flailing hands.

You're filth. You don't deserve to live, you filth.

The old man whimpered. The younger man cursed him.

A beating of several minutes. You thought it would cease, yet it continued. Such a deliberate beating can't be rushed, or careless. Even N. was staggering with exhaustion, he'd broken the ebony cane across a grave marker and flung both pieces at the fallen man in disgust.

When they left the cemetery, walking without haste on the graveled path, not wanting to attract attention on the graveled path, they checked another time and saw no one: Cross Memorial Cemetery was deserted.

From the parking lot, no one was visible in Cross Memorial Cemetery. Within a few hours the sun would sink beneath the horizon, for dusk came early at this time of year in Rochester, New York.

They drove to the hotel where they were *Mr. & Mrs.*

Eleventh floor of a high-rise building overlooking the interstate and already headlights were shining, out of the gathering darkness.

N.'s breath was still quickened, hoarse. She'd discovered that he was asthmatic, to a mild degree. As a boy, he'd suffered more seriously from the condition.

Wryly rubbing his knuckles. Though he'd worn thin leather gloves, yet his knuckles ached.

I hope you didn't h-hurt him badly. I hope . . .

God damn! I hope I did.

N. had opened the minibar. N. poured a tiny bottle of scotch into a glass for Ceille and a tiny bottle of scotch into a glass for himself. Laughing they struck the glasses together, hard. Ceille steeled herself, lifted the glass and swallowed.

They fell onto the absurd king-sized bed. The size of a football field as N. described it.

Drinking, and laughing. They were so happy suddenly.

N. kissed her, protruding his tongue into her mouth. She could not breathe, she was so very excited. The man kissed her breasts, her belly, he'd tugged open her clothing, she could not restrain him. In the cemetery G. was dying of an artery broken and bleeding into his brain. She seemed to know this. She was touching N.'s penis to guide it into her, or against her; gently nudging between her legs, the sweetest of caresses she felt with such intense pleasure, she could scarcely bear it. And he, the man, whose name she had forgotten in the exigency of the moment, shuddered and moaned in her arms as she held him, as tightly as her arms could clutch.

In the cemetery miles away the old man would not regain consciousness. The beautiful white hair was soaking with blood. The skull like an eggshell had been cracked and could not ever be repaired.

A trickle of sensation in her groin, she began to shudder, it came so strong. She shut her eyes seeing the trickle of blood seeping into the old man's brain. She would have wept except N. was kissing her mouth and his tongue filled her mouth.

No one will ever know she thought. *Our secret.*